Joel Baker

Friends of the Family

Copyright © 2009 Joel Baker
All rights reserved.

ISBN: 1-4392-5713-2
ISBN-13: 9781439257135

To order additional copies, please contact us.
BookSurge
www.booksurge.com
1-866-308-6235
orders@booksurge.com

DEDICATION

To my wife, Roxane, who actually thought I could write this and all my friends at Nextbigwriter.com, who helped to keep the light burning.

PROLOGUE

Grandpa Jesse was a hard man. Some people say he was a stone cold killer. Others say he did what he had to do; doing what was necessary to protect the family. It was a time when dying was easy and living was hard.

One thing everybody can agree on is that Jesse Colter loved his wife Sarah. He loved her, their kids, and those big awful dogs. Jesse and Sarah are long gone now. So are the dogs they brought with them to Haven. But their offspring are here, both the Colters and the dogs. Hard to explain, those dogs, doing what they do, giving everyone the willies and such.

If you're reading this, you probably know all about them dogs. We've had people come from as far away as fifty miles just to see them. They usually get back in their wagons shaking their heads wondering how such a thing could be. If you read Jesse's story you'll know.

My name is John Franklin Boyd. I'm the second son of Lily, Jesse and Sarah's only daughter. An old woman now, she's still the best healer around. That's the other reason folks come to visit Haven. First they want to see them dogs, and then mama for poultices and remedies to cure their ills.

I build wagons, big strong wagons that can carry anything. I built every wagon in Haven and for miles around. Wagons for hauling produce and hay mostly. It's said none of my wagons has ever left the valley. That's because no one leaves our valley except to find a wife. Then they always come back with a wife, and sometimes with a new baby too.

This way of living may seem normal to you. I doubt if any of you actually lived during the go-back. That's what we call the time when Jesse's story begins. Grandpa Jesse, Sarah, and the folks their age used to tell us about the time before go-back.

It was a strange time. It was a time of cars, and trains and televisions. Lights came on when you turned a switch. People could fly in aero planes anywhere they wanted. Nobody had to chop wood or many of the things we do every day. Horses were a hobby for rich folk and not for plowing or getting from one place to another.

Everybody went to school. They bought food at big stores and never had to turn a spade of earth. Those stores had racks of clothes you could walk right in and buy. Everybody wore shoes that were made of canvas and just threw them away when they got worn or dirty. Hard to believe; but the old people all said it was true.

Nobody seems to really know what happened to cause the go-back. They say it was sudden. The oil they used for all this stuff ran out or something. Banks failed. So did everything else. All we do know for sure is that in a few weeks things just stopped working. Then they had riots. It wasn't long before they were killing each other for one reason or another. Then they started killing for no reason at all.

People got terrible sick and died. Some said other people caused it. Others said we did it to ourselves. The country fell apart. So did all the other countries. Then everybody started hoarding food and such. Some people became scavengers, living on what they could steal by taking from other people. Some really bad people gathered these scavengers into gangs. Then things got really ugly. There was talk of cannibalism, people eating other people, and other horrors too terrible to imagine. The land emptied as people died or were killed. It was as though people forgot how to fend for themselves. Some just gave up hope and quit.

It was worse up north than here in Tennessee. In the rural part of the south we weren't as far from the land. People used to make fun of us. They called us hicks and red necks. Now we're here and they're gone. It was like everyone forgot which end of a shovel to use. They kept waiting around for the government or someone to come take care of them. Nobody came. That was true all over, just less so here.

I first heard the story of Jesse and Sarah when I was a little boy. I heard it many times since. Jesse was an old man by then and his Sarah was gone. But his mind was still sharp. People still came to Jesse for advice. His stories were sought after, in spite of his somewhat rambling style. Whenever it stormed or snowed, or the children just got bored, the cry would go up.

"Tell us the story, Grandpa Jesse. Tell us the story!"

Jesse would always protest and grumble, muttering under his breath. "There's too much work to do to be fooling around with all this nonsense." But the gleam in his eye would give it all away. He would wait for all us children to gather in front of the fire, quiet and still, with our legs drawn up to our chests and eyes wide with the waiting.

Jesse would look at each of us and begin the story always in the same way. "It seems just like yesterday…"

***

Some time ago I found Jesse and Sarah's story all written down. It was in a dusty old pine box, under some old tarps, way in the back of a shed. A small rose was carved into the lid of the box. I read the story and it's the same one Grandpa Jesse use to tell.

I want to warn you it's a bit gritty. Those were tough times they lived through and not easy to hear about. I don't know who wrote it down. But it's a story that needs told. Was Jesse a stone cold killer? Before you go judging Jesse one way or the other, you should hear the real story.

chapter 1

THE CROSS HAIRS of the scope rested comfortably on the young boy's forehead. Jesse Colter felt his heart's rhythm increase as he swept his field of fire over the scene below.

An old man knelt by a stricken form lying on the ground. A boy and a teenaged girl leaned over the body, as the old man apparently searched the pockets for food or anything of use. All three wore tattered rags and a hunted look. The steam of their breath hovered above the deadly scene.

"Dad, I got the old man," Mark, Jesse's fifteen-year-old son whispered next to him. Both Jesse and Mark lay side by side in the snow on a small knoll some fifty yards from the group of scavengers clustered below.

"Wait for the signal, and concentrate on your breathing," Jesse whispered in return. Jesse didn't want Mark hyperventilating like the last time. It had gone badly when Mark had gut shot the scavenger, rather than a clean kill.

Jesse glanced at the slate sky spitting the occasional snow flake. The clouds appeared to be lowering by the minute. It looked like it would get a lot worse and soon. Still, he wasn't convinced these particular scavengers needed killing. He waited and watched their actions.

"Dad...Dad...Do you see what I see?" Mark whispered as softly as he could.

Jesse moved the scope back to the old man and saw the knife appear in his hand. It looked like some sort of steak knife with a serrated edge. The blade was bent at an odd angle. The girl reached behind her and set a large blackened metal cooking pot next to the cadaver. The boy began clapping his dirty hands, hopping from one leg to another like a demented elf.

All three seemed to be suffering from a similar disease, their faces covered in seeping sores. The color of the sickness didn't look like the normal pox they'd dealt with before, but from this distance it was hard to tell for sure. What Jesse knew was this group was a danger on several levels. After several moments, Jesse looked around and made the decision.

"Hey, kid. You ok?" Jesse asked.

"Sure Dad. Let's just get this over with."

"You take the old man," Jesse said, moving his scope to the elf, "whenever you're ready. Don't forget to breathe slowly."

The crack of Mark's rifle seemed loud. Jesse tightened his finger and felt the recoil of his rifle against his shoulder. The elf's arms flew gracefully over his head as he toppled backwards into a ditch.

Jesse quickly positioned the crosshairs of his scope to the forehead of the girl. At first she seemed confused. She looked around dumfounded for several seconds, her mouth open as she watched the old man and boy jerk backward. She glanced up towards where Mark and Jesse lay in the brush on the elevated rise some distance from where she stood. Her dirty, tattered coat was open, in spite of the cold. She raised her right hand and brushed a wisp of hair from her eyes. It almost appeared to Jesse as if she waved.

Jesse pulled the trigger.

The crack of his rifle echoed off the hillside then returned to silence. The acrid smell of gunpowder mixed with the crisp clean freshness of falling snowflakes. Vapors of steam rose from the weeds marking the spot where the bodies lay in a cold sleep.

Jesse held his hand out motioning Mark to stay where he was. He listened intently for the telltale roar of engines. Gasoline was more precious than gold. Large bands of scavengers frequently sent the weaker members out on foot to for whatever they could find. Just like the three in the snow down below. They used them as bait hoping that someone would take a chance and reveal their position. People who took chances died quickly and without comment.

Jesse finally got to his feet and peered through the thickening snow. He felt tired and alone. It had been a year of kill or be killed. Twelve months of watching friends, relatives, and neighbors die. Overnight the whole country regressed two hundred years. Food, heat, light, water, medicine, police, and everything else just failed. Everything and everyone forced to go back to a time of desperate survival.

"Let's go home", Jesse said.

"Do you think they were loners?" Mark asked as he scrambled off the rise.

"I don't know, but I think so," Jesse replied. "They were in bad shape even for scavengers."

Friends of the Family

Jesse watched his son and was again reminded of how much Mark resembled Jesse's own father. He was tall for his age and had his grandpa's sandy blond hair. If Mark resembled Jesse at all, it was the way he walked. He had the same long strides and comfortable gait as Jesse.

Jesse turned and joined Mark walking single file, until they passed the edge of what remained of the town of Liberty Ohio. Smoke rose from the few occupied houses remaining. The pervasive pungent smell of burning wood hung in the air. Jesse and his son approached the silent center of town, they stopping in the road, listening to the desolate sound of the wind whistling through the dead power lines. Suddenly Jesse tensed, looking first left and then right.

"What's wrong?" Mark whispered.

"Nothing, I guess. I thought I heard something," Jesse replied as he studied the empty houses staring back at him through vacant windows.

"Are you still thinking about moving us to Tennessee?" Mark asked as he shouldered his rifle.

"Yeah, but we got to see what your Mom says. The truck and fuel are still at the garage. I'm going to talk with her tonight about it." Jesse knew he'd been lucky to have just filled the diesel fuel storage tanks at his business when everything failed.

A cholera epidemic hit the town hard a few weeks later. Rumors of how far the epidemic spread were passed on by the occasional straggler.

Sarah's parents were among the first to die. Jesse and Sarah quarantined their family as they fought to survive. When they finally emerged, most of the people of Liberty had fled or were dead. Those remaining came together long enough to bury them, and then retreated back into their houses.

Jesse knew it would be difficult for Sarah to leave the place where her parents were buried. She was devastated by their loss. Liberty was the only place she'd ever lived. But he knew they had to get to Haven.

Why should we go back to Tennessee?"

"Hopefully so we don't have to do this anymore, Mark. I know those people. They're tough and resilient. Someplace we can stop looking over our shoulder and look to our future instead. I just hope we haven't waited too long." Jesse knew Mark was also dealing with the unknown. He also knew they should have packed up and left last fall instead of waiting.

Friends of the Family

Mark nodded his head and smiled. "I'm sold. There's nothing keeping us here. But, good luck convincing Mom."

Jesse looked around as the snow seemed to strengthen. The wind whipped down empty streets forming drifts in the gutters. He felt the sting on his cheeks and hid his face from the wind as his eyes began to water. Just as Jesse wiped tears from his eyes, he saw Mark drop to a crouch and whip his rifle to his shoulder. Jesse dropped to one knee, instantly alert, his rifle raised. "What is it?"

"Dogs, I think. A bunch of them just ran through that alley on the left."

Mark pointed towards the old pharmacy and cleaners on the corner. Jesse sprinted to the corner and peeked up the alley. Wild dogs were a growing problem. They were more successful than their owners at adapting. Even so, food was getting scarce and the packs were getting bolder. Jesse returned to where Mark now rested.

"We better send Cole to deal with the dogs," Jesse said.

"I can do it."

"I know you can, but Cole's really good at taking care of dogs. It's difficult to take out a whole pack of them. Some always seem to get away. I want them all dead."

Jesse knew Mark was disappointed, but felt Cole, Mark's childhood friend, was very close to going as feral as the dogs he hunted. He was rail thin, with a strange dead cast to his eyes. From a distance he appeared normal enough. Up close, Cole had ancient, tired eyes. He was driven. Jesse thought his demons were somehow understandable.

Cole had watched a mob beat his father to death with a tire iron for a few gallons of gas when the go-back started. Since then, Cole was a strange boy, living on his own. He would stop by the Colter house for a meal now and then. Jesse, who also was orphaned at a young age, felt empathy for the boy.

Jesse and his son headed off towards home. "Don't say anything to the family about this morning. It will just upset them."

"I know, Dad. Besides, I think I know who those scavengers were after. It was Mr. Warner, wasn't it?" Mark said with a catch in his voice.

"It looked like him," Jesse replied.

"Do you think they killed him?"

"I don't know, maybe Jacob got careless, or his heart gave out. He was an old guy with a bad ticker. But who knows? That's why I keep telling you to stay alert. You can't afford to get careless."

"I know, Dad, I know."

"I'll try to get back out there tomorrow and bring Jacob back into town," Jesse said, "We owe him at least a burial." The snow slowed as Jesse studied the concerned look on his son's face. He was more resolved than ever to get the family back to Tennessee and Haven.

chapter 2

THE SNOW STOPPED late in the day. Sarah stepped out on the front porch. She wrapped a white shawl that had belonged to her mother tightly around her shoulders. She spotted Jesse and Mark walking past the trees in the front yard and up the driveway. Their rifles were cradled in their arms.

From the looks on their faces she knew that the day had not gone well. Sarah waved and smiled as Jesse took off his stocking cap and scratched his head. Wool always made his head itch. "You two better get in the house before you freeze to death. Are you done for the day?"

"All done," Jesse replied.

"Go wash up. Dinners almost ready," Sarah called.

They continued up the driveway. Sarah went back inside and looked out the dining room window. She saw Jesse laugh and give Mark a playful punch in the arm as they walked behind the house. The metal on metal squeak of the hand pump went on for some time as first Jesse, and then Mark worked the handle. It sent shivers down Sarah's back like fingernails on a chalk board. Finally the noise stopped.

Mark and Jesse had found the hand water pump in an old hardware store. They'd driven the well by hand after they'd lost water pressure. They'd hit water at thirty five feet, but Jesse had insisted they go deeper. Sarah was convinced that the deeper well had saved their lives. They'd managed to avoid getting sick when the sewage treatment plant outside of town had failed and contaminated the ground water. A cholera epidemic had raged out of control shortly thereafter.

Sarah sat in the dining room and listened to the quiet. It was a silence broken only by the ghostly whine of the wind blowing through the eaves and the occasional groan of an old house. She felt the chill of the still room and wondered if she'd ever really be warm again. It had been a long cold winter and Sarah was tired. The light through the window was fading. She stood and began moving about the dining room lighting kerosene lamps. She trimmed each wick, lit the lamp, and replaced the glass cover.

She looked up as Jesse and Mark walked through the side door. Jesse handed his rifle to Mark to clean, then stomped the snow off his feet. He laid his gloves on the wood stove in the back of the house. The sizzle of melting snow and smell of wet wool hung in the air. The table was set and cooking smells came from the kitchen.

"Hey, sweetheart," Jesse said with a smile.

"Hey, yourself," Sarah smiled in return.

Jesse took three giant steps across the dining room and swept her into his arms. Sarah hugged his neck closely. He smelled of pine needles, smoke and the cold. As they embraced, he whispered into her ear. "How come the worse it gets, the better you look?"

"I'm not even sure that's a compliment!" she said, pushing back from Jesse and slapping him on the shoulder. "Put me down and go take your dirty boots off."

"Done and done," he replied setting her gently on her feet and laughing.

Sarah turned as Mark came into the room. "Mark, go get your brother and sister. It's time for dinner."

"Hey! You guys! Come and get it!" Mark yelled.

"Thanks, Mark, I could have done that," she commented shaking her head. She had to remind herself that Mark was only fifteen. So tall, and asked to do so much, she thought.

Two minutes later, Paul and Lily thumped down the stairs and raced for the table. Paul had turned thirteen in December and Lily was eight. Sarah placed the typical assortment of food dishes on the table and sat next to Jesse.

Sarah thought dinner went well. Mark seemed especially quiet. The complaints about having to eat canned stewed tomatoes every night were the same. Jesse and Mark had found cases and cases of the stuff in the basement of Shamrock Supermarket.

They'd salvaged what they could find from abandoned houses. Everything from cans of corn, vegetables, coffee, tomatoes, and green beans to jars of pickles. Tonight she'd added a can of mushroom soup to the green beans for flavor. Sarah had three cans of Spam stashed away for special occasions.

Friends of the Family

After dinner, Mark and Paul disappeared upstairs. Sarah looked up at the ceiling where, judging from the thumping coming through the ceiling, a wrestling match had just broken out. Lily sat at one end of the table, worrying over a book.

"Lily? Honey, why don't you run upstairs and do your reading? Your mom and I want to talk," Jesse said.

"Okay, Daddy."

Sarah wondered what this was about. Jesse had seemed deep in thought during dinner. She watched Lily thump her way up the stairs and waited for the inevitable yell. "Will you guys cut it out? I'm trying to read!" The thumping slowed, but only marginally.

"I'll get us some coffee", Sarah said, walking into the kitchen and picking up the coffee pot from the wood stove. "Damn! The pot's almost empty. You can have this and I'll make some more."

She emptied the dregs of the coffee pot into Jesse's cup and sat down next to him. Jesse took a sip and looked up at her. He thought for a few moments before breaking the silence.

"I think it's time to make some plans for what we're going to do this spring," he started.

"OK. I'm listening," Sarah said as she stood and walked towards the kitchen. She felt Jesse watching her. She glanced back over her shoulder and with a flirty smile said, "What you looking at, mister?"

Jesse grinned. "I never get tired of watching you walk away."

Sarah stuck her tongue out at him, and disappeared through the kitchen door with an exaggerated swing of her hips. She first poured the water from the kettle on the stove over the dishes and left them to soak. Then she filled the coffee pot and set it on the burner. She dried her hands and went back and sat by Jesse, a worried look on her face. "What plans Jesse?"

"I think it's time for us to get out of here."

"Where would we go?"

"Haven," Jesse said.

A flood of memories clouded Sarah's mind. It had been some time since they'd visited Jesse's childhood home. A beautiful little valley just northwest of Chattanooga, Haven had been abandoned shortly after Jesse's parents were killed in a car crash. She and Jesse had visited Haven several times over the past ten years. The buildings were always the same, same road leading back to the valley, everything so overgrown. It had been getting more and more difficult just to find it. Jesse and Sarah had gone through all the buildings, the house, the barn, and sheds. Everything covered with dust. The tools still hung on the walls. It had a really an odd, almost creepy feeling of abandonment about it.

Sarah hadn't been impressed with the nearby town of Eagle Rock either. A rough crowd had stood around and stared at them and she'd felt uneasy the whole time they were there. Jesse managed to locate Franklin and Hattie Pierce, the couple who had looked after Jesse for a while after his parents' accident. Franklin and Hattie had worked for Jesse's father on the farm. Both seemed to have aged well.

Franklin had told Jesse that he and Hattie were thinking of moving. They'd encountered trouble from time to time with some of the local toughs. Apparently he and Hattie kept to themselves as much as possible. Jesse had suggested they move out to Haven and look after the place. Everyone seemed pleased with the offer. They'd spent the next couple of days helping them move and cleaning the old place.

"Haven, Jesse? Are you sure?" Sarah asked. "It's such a long way away. I know its bad here, but Tennessee seems so far away."

Jesse took another sip of coffee and appeared in deep thought. There was silence for several moments except for the occasional soft thud coming through the dining room ceiling. "I don't think we have a choice. We've waited over a year for someone to show up and fix things. Well, they're not coming."

"If I thought we had half a chance of getting away from this hell hole, we could leave tomorrow. But it's got to be three hundred miles. Jesse, how can we take the children that far? What makes you think it's safer in Tennessee? I mean, we don't know what's waiting for us there."

"Sarah, this town, this whole part of the country is dying. Scavengers, sickness, everything's changed and we need to change too. I think we have to pick a spot. Some place with some land to grow food. Make a decent place where our kids and our grandkids can grow up."

"But why move to Tennessee?"

"I think the people down there probably came through this better. Certainly, East Tennessee would have. That part of the country didn't even get electricity until the TVA came through in the thirties. We didn't get phone lines at Haven until the fifties. Besides, we know

Friends of the Family

people there. People like Hattie and Franklin who will welcome us."

Sarah sat silent, thinking. The sound of the grandfather clock ticked away, and the silence from upstairs indicated the wrestling match was over. "Okay, Jesse, I think you're right about it being time to leave. But there's something else."

"What?" Jesse asked looking concerned.

"I know what you and Mark have to do out there, on the perimeter. We don't talk about it, but I know. I'm worried about Paul now. He's beginning to feel left out. Every time you and Mark head out the door, Paul just mopes around. He feels he's old enough to go with you. I'm afraid it's just a matter of time before you'll need him to help as well."

"Oh Sarah, I don't think…"

"Just promise me you won't get Paul involved in all this, if you can avoid it. Maybe you could teach him some things when it isn't so dangerous. Spend more time with him. Promise me?"

"I promise, sweetheart," Jesse replied.

The clock ticked and the house was silent as Sarah and Jesse both sat thinking about what lay ahead.

"Honey, do you really think we can do this?" Sarah asked after several minutes.

"Sure we can. We love each other and that's a really good place to start. I think we need to dig down deep. But we can do it. You know why?"

"Why?"

"Cause we have to. That's why."

Sarah got up, came around the table in the flickering lamplight, put her arms around Jesse's head and hugged him tightly. She felt the back of Jesse's head press gently into the soft warmth of her breasts.

"Let's do it, Jesse," Sarah whispered in his ear. "I've always trusted you to do the right thing. We've been sitting here hoping someone else would make things right, that the lights would magically come back on. Maybe the government would finally show up and arrest all the bad guys. Well, it's not going to happen. It's time for us to make things right."

"I love you, Sarah," Jesse whispered back.

Sarah smiled down at Jesse and kissed him deeply. She sensed a rising interest in Jesse, but still had some questions. "When do we leave, and how are we going to get to Haven?" Sarah asked, breaking the moment.

Jesse seemed distracted, but came back to the topic. "Ah, well, I think we have to wait until spring. The truck still works, I've got enough diesel fuel stashed away to get us there. I'm just not sure what the roads are like. Worse case, if the truck breaks down, we'll have to walk. I think you and the boys can do it, but I worry about Lily, especially in the winter."

"It's over three hundred miles isn't it?" Sarah asked.

"More like three hundred and sixty, and we'll have to stick to the back roads. Hopefully the bridges over the Ohio are intact and open."

"How long do you think it will take?"

"We should plan on making ten miles a day. I figure thirty days."

"Are you sure it will take a whole month, Jesse?"

"No, I'm not sure. But I think we should plan for the worst. As long as we stick together, we'll be all right. I just hope Franklin and Hattie are still looking after the place and are ready for some company."

Sarah sat and watched Jesse making lists of things they would need to take with them. She knew this was Jesse's way of organizing his thoughts. Later, after she made sure the kids were in bed, she began to feel tired. "I'm going to get ready for bed, don't be too long okay?"

"I'll be right up, sweetheart," Jessie replied.

Sarah went into the kitchen, washed up, put on her nightgown, and then went upstairs and crawled into bed. A short time later she heard Jesse on the stairs, and as he entered their bedroom she heard Jesse kick something.

"Damn, that hurts!" Jesse exclaimed as he got under the blankets.

"What happened?"

"I tripped over that stupid rocking chair again."

"Aw. that's too bad," Sarah said, "Want me to kiss it and make it all better?"

Late that night, Sarah lay in bed still feeling the serenity of having made love. She shuddered with the spasm of remembrance. In the back of her mind she thought about a baby and what that would mean. She knew it was in God's hands but worried about it none the less.

Sarah also thought about Jacob Warner. Jesse had told her about that nice old man now dead by the side of the road. She thought about how poor old Jacob deserved better. But then, so did her parents and everybody else. Even the scavengers deserved better. It just wasn't right. People were killing each other over a pack of matches or a can of soup.

    Sarah rolled over and drifted into sleep.

chapter 3

Jesse bolted upright in bed, muscles and the cords in his neck stretched taut. All he could remember from the nightmare that woke him were images of the bodies by the road outside of town. They looked dead, but were sitting upright in the snow. As he approached, they all turned and stared at him. There was a metal kettle sitting in front of them. The girl slowly stirred whatever was in the pot. She smiled at Jesse.

It was morning. Sarah had already gone down stairs. Still unnerved, He tried to gather his thoughts. It had seemed so real. Even though he knew it was a dream, Jesse still felt something was wrong. He was anxious to get Jacob back to town and get rid of the scavengers.

Downstairs, everything was normal. Jesse kissed Sarah and checked on the kids and found them already hard at their studies. He headed out to the enclosed back porch, shrugged into his white and brown camouflaged coat and insulated boots. He grabbed a coil of rope and looped it through his belt. His rifle, a British made SA80 with a mounted sniper scope, stood next to the back door.

The rifle had been stuffed way in the back of the counter of Bud McCann's gun store. Jesse had wondered at the time what Bud had wanted with a high powered sniper's weapon. It was curious. He checked to make sure that the thirty round ammo clip was full and snapped it into to the breech. As he stepped outside, he moved the safety to off, chambered a round, and headed into the bitter wind blowing up the driveway.

Every day Jesse walked the perimeter of the town. Some days Mark went with him. Most times nothing happened. Occasionally, like yesterday, something did. Initially, the town had organized constant patrols and checkpoints. But as people ran away or died, those left lost interest in everything but surviving. Jesse kept at it because he thought it was important. He wasn't sure it did much good.

Friends of the Family

Jesse saw smoke coming from the Palmer place. Larry Palmer wasn't someone he would have picked as a likely survivor. Larry seemed like a decent sort, but was a bit on the lazy side and badly out of shape. Jesse walked up the driveway. "Larry!" Jesse called. "It's me, Jesse!"

A minute went by and the house appeared to wink as a curtain quickly opened and closed. Larry Palmer walked out on his porch and waved.

"How's it going, big guy?" Larry asked.

"Pretty good, how are you doing?" Jesse recalled how Larry and his wife Estelle had retired to Liberty to enjoy the peace and quiet.

"Me and the wife are thinking about moving on next spring. How about you?" Larry asked.

"We're not sure yet. What direction you heading?"

"West, I believe. We were thinking about looking up the in-laws, over near Hudson in Southern Illinois. We heard from them about six months ago and they were doing alright."

"Sounds good," Jesse said not sure at all if either Larry or Estelle could make it to the county line, let alone Illinois. "By the way, we came across some scavengers yesterday. I thought you ought to know."

"Did you take care of them?" Larry asked.

"I didn't have much of a choice. They were sick and seemed like a crazy bunch."

"You don't have to explain to me, Jesse. Ain't no one done more for the people around here."

"There's bad news too, Larry. They got Jacob Warner," Jesse said, looking down.

"Damn! I really liked the old guy."

"I know. He kept to himself, but Jacob was a good guy," Jesse said. "Listen, I'm going to head back out by the water plant road and bring Jacob back to town. Thought I'd put him in City Hall until the spring thaw with the rest of them."

"You want me to go with you?" Larry asked, sounding less than enthusiastic and a little whiney. Jesse thought if Larry went with him, he'd have to drag both Jacob and Larry back.

"No thanks, I can get him," Jesse said. "He's been out there all night, so he should be frozen stiff as a board. I'll just tie a rope on his ankles and drag him back."

"Well, let me know if you want help."

"Good luck with finding the in-laws in Illinois."

Friends of the Family

Jesse waved as he walked back down the drive. A half-hour later he spotted the turnoff he and mark had used yesterday. As Jesse neared the top of the rise, the sun came out cold in the January sky. Most of the tracks from yesterday were gone, covered by blowing snow and drifts. Jesse lowered himself and crawled to a point where he could see the scene below.

Something was different.

Jesse waited a few minutes and walked down to where Jacob's body lay covered with a dusting of snow. The bodies of the three scavengers were gone. He walked in a circle looking for signs of who had taken them. The pot and bent knife still lay by Jacob. Jesse dropped the coil of rope. Ten feet from Jacob's corpse, he saw faint tire tracks nearly covered up by drifting snow. They led west, away from town. He decided he better follow them.

The wind was blowing snow in Jesse's face, and covering his tracks as soon as he made them. Jesse approached a curve in the road and heard voices coming in his direction. He jumped quickly to the right side of the road, doing his best to cover his tracks as he went. Jesse couched in the brush with a clear view. He brought his rifle forward and waited.

Three men carrying shotguns came into view walking side by side. They were huddled over with the cold, and appeared more concerned with keeping warm then watching where they were going. Soon they were close enough for Jesse to overhear their conversation.

"Boy, the Chief is pissed big time!" man one said.

"Big deal. He's always pissed about one thing or another," man two replied.

"Do you think he's going to want to take out that little town up ahead?" man three asked.

"The way those three gimps we found yesterday bought it? No way. That was stone cold. All three shot right between the eyes," man two replied.

"Chief thinks it's too risky," man one said. All three men stopped, and then turned and headed back to where Jesse lay hidden in the brush.

"Chief's a pussy. He sits in that warm house with all his god damn buddies while we're out here freezing," man two said.

"He told me we might be heading back west. Thinks there might still be easy pickings that way," man three said.

Friends of the Family

"There damn well better be. I'm coming down with a bad case of blue balls, and not just from the cold!" man two said. The men disappeared back around the curve, laughing.

Jesse waited a few more minutes as the laughter receded. He returned to the road and stood for a minute or two listening. That was way too close. He made a mental note to keep an eye on this bunch for the next few days. In fact, he should send Cole out just to make sure.

Jesse left Jacob's body in the jury box of the main court room in City Hall. He would sit with the others waiting for the spring thaw or judgment day, which ever came first. It was a short three blocks to his old garage. He walked up to the front door of his old office, turned the key, and entered the dark, musty-smelling building. It was odd to be here alone. He imagined he could still hear his work crew laughing and talking in the back areas.

He meandered through the cavernous building, making sure the truck was still sitting undisturbed, covered by a brown canvas drop cloth. The large boxy truck weighed just over six tons. It had a small living area so construction crews could stay at a work site until a job was done. It was designed to house two men comfortably, or three in a pinch. A window connected the living area to the cab. The back third of the truck was for storage and contained a mini-shop complete with workbenches. Jesse planned to remove everything but the benches.

Once he had checked on the truck, Jesse returned to his office. He sat down at his old desk, and out of habit, picked up the telephone to see if it had a dial tone. Like everything else the phone was dead. Jesse wondered what he would have done if there had been a dial tone.

He looked up and spotted the framed check hanging on the wall. It was the first check made out to his new company, thirty two dollars and twelve cents. He had fixed a window for Jim Handley at his hardware store. Sarah had decided to frame the check, even though at the time, they weren't really sure how they would pay next month's rent.

He and Sarah's celebration that night had resulted in a baby boy. When Mark was four years old, he'd ask his mother where he came from. Sarah told him he'd come from Handley Hardware. Jesse smiled as he locked the door and walked away headed towards home.

That evening Jesse asked Mark to help carry more of the neighbor's house up the driveway before they lost all daylight. They threw the last of the rafters on the pile of lumber. Both sat on the edge of the front porch in the gathering darkness and rested.

"I haven't seen Cole for a few days, Mark. I'm starting to worry about him. Have you seen him around?" Jesse asked.

Mark laughed. "You've got to be kidding. I see him all the time."

"Around here?"

"I see him all the time."

"Yeah, sure you do. Just yell out when you see him next time," Jesse said.

"He's under those pine trees right now," Mark said in a low voice.

Jesse glanced towards the tall pine trees clustered in the corner of their yard. He saw a figure crouched by the trunks low beneath the limbs.

"The third tree down?" Jesse asked.

"That's him."

"Why don't you go see if you can get Cole to join us for supper? He's probably hungry from sitting under that tree."

"Gees, do I have to? He gives me the creeps. He never talks, he's always sneaking around, and when he looks at you, well, it's like nobody's home."

"Well, I think he's lonely. I think he remembers when you were friends, and he hangs around just to be close to us. We probably remind him of his family. I'd like for you to go invite him for supper."

Jesse got up and walked into the house. He looked out the window and saw Mark get up and walk towards the pine trees that lined the front yard.

After dinner, Jesse invited Cole and Mark outside for a talk. The sun was down and the temperature dropping fast. The moon appeared in the darkened sky and the silver light glistened off of the snow. The crunch of the snow on a bitter cold night accented the cloud of steam hanging in the still air from their breath.

"Cole, we spotted some dogs running across the alley by the hardware store yesterday. Did you see any sign of them?"

"Yeah, I saw them a few days ago. I know where they been staying too."

"Where?" Mark asked.

"They're living under the old pharmacy by Handley's hardware. Someone must have left the outside cellar door open," Cole said.

"Can you take care of them?" Jesse asked.

"Sure. I've just been trying to figure out how best to go about it. See, them dogs are too well fed. There must be five or six adults and a litter of pups."

"What do you mean 'too well fed'?" Mark asked, stomping his feet against the cold.

Cole glanced at Mark. "I snuck up on them outside the hardware store. The pups were out and playing tug of war with a red flannel shirt."

"So?" Mark asked.

"There was an arm in one sleeve," Cole said, looking away from Mark and Jesse. The answer hung frozen in the brittle air.

"Cole, some scavengers are camped west of town. Don't take those dogs out or do anything to attract attention until they leave," Jesse said.

"They're gone, Mr. Colter. I watched them leave late this afternoon, heading west. Sorry looking bunch too. There must have been seven or eight or them. They had a rattletrap pickup truck. Something else you should know," Cole said. "The scavengers left some stuff that makes me think they'll be back. It looked like a stash to me."

Jesse looked at the moon and watched the clouds skitter across the face thinking that they might have to move up the time table. "Did you go through the stuff they left?"

"Not yet. I'll take a run out there tomorrow," Cole said.

"Good. Make sure everything we can't use is destroyed. In fact, burn the place to the ground. No reason to leave anything for them to come back to," Jesse said. He and Sarah were still uncertain if they should tell Cole about their plans to leave. "Do you have a warm place to sleep tonight? You're welcome to stay with us."

Mark glanced quickly at his dad, and then looked away.

"Sure do," Cole replied.

"Do you need help with the dogs?"

"Naw, I got it covered. Thanks for the meal, Mr. Colter. See you later Mark," Cole said with a smile as he headed down the driveway.

Jesse stood for a few moments thinking about Cole's smile as he watched him disappear around the corner. He thought there was something unnatural about that smile. Then it hit him. It was Cole's eyes. They were the eyes of an old man. They were the eyes of Jacob Warner.

chapter 4

Jesse stood on the front porch watching the weather rapidly deteriorate. The first week of February had brought with it a false spring thaw. Breezes had softened and warmed melting most of the snow. Winter was now returning with a vengeance. The temperature had dropped twenty degrees in the past two hours, and the snow was beginning to spit again.

Everyone was anxious to get on the road. Jesse and the boys had made another pass through town to check all the empty buildings for canned goods, guns, ammunition, or anything else they could use. They'd found nothing. Jesse glanced over and saw Sarah had joined him on the porch.

"How goes the sorting?" Jesse asked. Sarah and Lily were sifting through the family's possessions for what would be loaded into the truck and what stayed.

Sarah did not appear happy. "We've got a system, but this is just impossible."

"What system?"

"Well, we made three stacks. One is the 'Goes' pile, the second's the 'Stays' pile, and the third's the 'Shouldn't Go, but I just can't bear to Leave It' pile."

"What's the problem?"

"Everything is ending up in the third pile."

Jesse laughed. "The truck's about finished. Why don't you come and take a look at it?"

"I don't know. Just not enough hours in the day, I guess. Maybe I'll try to later," Sarah said, stepping back towards the door. "Are you coming in?"

Jesse looked up at the snow as the wind picked up. "Not just yet. I think I'll go for a walk around town. Is Mark inside?"

"I'll send him out. Do you have anything Paul can do? He's driving Lily and me crazy."

"Sure. Have him start cutting wood to length for the stoves."

By the time Jesse and Mark returned from their walk the snow had really picked up. Paul seemed upset about being left at the house, so Jesse and Mark spent the rest of the afternoon helping Paul keep the snow from burying their well pump and stacking wood next to the house.

That night the kids fell asleep in front of the stove in the living room. Outside it continued to snow. The bitter wind howled as the snow whirled and cascaded into drifts. Sarah and Jesse stood with an arm around each other's waist and gazed out of the window at the deepening snow.

"This is some storm isn't it?" Sarah asked.

"I just hope it's one of the last. I'm really concerned about getting out of here. I'm worried about Cole too. What's going to happen to him when we leave?"

"I think we should ask him to go with us," Sarah spoke softly after a long time.

"Me too," Jesse said. "I hate the thought of leaving him here all alone. I think he's getting better too."

"That may be wishful thinking by both of us. But I agree. We can't leave him here all by himself," Sarah said. "You talk to him. See if he wants leave with us."

Jesse nodded. The wind moaned through the eaves sending a shiver down his spine.

***

The rest of that week crept by with more snow and cold. Chopping wood and fetching water kept Jesse and the boys busy. Finally, the snow stopped and the sun came out with a cold glare. Jesse knew his talk with Paul was overdue. Jesse took his rifle and called Mark and Paul outside.

"Paul, would you like to go with us on our walk today?"

"You bet!" Paul said.

"Go get your rifle and let's go," Jesse said. Paul raced for the house.

"Are you and mom sure about this, Dad?" Mark asked as Paul tore through the door into the house.

"Your Mom understands Paul is getting older and wants to be a part of what we do. If we look after him, he'll be alright. We'll go slow and stay away from the more dangerous areas."

Paul raced out of the house and Jesse made sure he was focused on the fact he was carrying a loaded weapon. They'd walked about three blocks when Jesse stopped in the middle of the snowy street. He slowly scanned the empty houses.

"What's wrong, Dad?" Paul asked.

"I'm not sure Paul, maybe nothing. I want you to work on being quiet and listening. We all need to learn to be more aware of what's going on around us. Our lives may depend on your ability to spot something out of place, not quite right," Jesse said. "Now look around and tell me if anything appears out place."

Paul studied the houses and street for signs.

"Well, did you spot anything?" Jesse asked.

Paul raised his hand. "I noticed footprints in the snow from that house to the next one." Paul pointed at a house across from where they stood.

"You don't have to raise your hand, Paul. What else?"

"It looks like the tracks skipped the houses that look lived in," Paul smiled proudly.

"Mark, what does that tell you?" Jesse asked.

"It tells me Cole's been out sneaking around," Mark said, smiling.

"You might be right," Jesse said. "But if your mother's and Lily's life depended on it, and they just might, how sure are you that those prints are Cole's?"

Mark looked a little embarrassed and nodded his head.

"Good. Now come with me," Jesse said, as he walked over to the prints in the snow followed by the two boys. Jesse bent over and looked closely. Mark and Paul did the same.

"Okay, guys. What do you see?"

Both Mark and Paul hesitated. Finally Mark said, "There are two different sets of footprints".

"What makes you think so?"

"They're different sizes."

"What else?"

"They're headed in the same direction?" Paul ventured.

"What else?" Jesse asked. Both boys studied the footprints intently as Jesse waited. Neither boy could find anything else.

"In order to see, you've got to look," Jesse finally said. "Here's what I see. Two men, one large one small, walked this way. One was Cole, and he was tracking the big guy. The big guy came by the day before yesterday, and Cole followed his tracks yesterday. The big guy was hurt."

"How can you tell all that?" Mark asked.

"Well, first look closely at the two sets of prints," Jesse explained. "The bigger set's pressed deeper in the snow. We know the big guy's a lot heavier. I know the smaller set's Cole because I marked the bottom of his shoes. Look closely. See that little X mark where the tread shows up in the smaller print? I cut that

Friends of the Family

X myself. Take a minute and look closely at the bottom of your own shoes. Do it now."

Both boys sat, and peered at the bottom of their shoes.

"I see it. I got three little dashes up by the toe," Mark said.

"I got four little dashes on mine," Paul chimed in.

"That's right boys, and your mother has two dashes and my shoe's marked with one dash. When I was young, my friends and I used to track each other as a game, in the woods. I used to mark their shoes when they didn't know it. That way, I could always look at a print and tell whose it was. It may be important, so remember it."

Mark thought for a minute. "Lily has five dashes doesn't she?"

"You got it, Mark," Jesse said with some satisfaction.

"Didn't your friends think that was cheating?" Paul asked.

"I never told them and they thought I was part Indian. It was a definite advantage," Jesse said. "But Paul, I want you to take this to heart. This is no game. It's serious business. One of us could get hurt or killed. On our trip we may meet some really bad guys, maybe some good ones too. But until we can know one way or another, we have to assume they're all bad. No exceptions."

"How did you know that Cole was tracking the big guy, and when they came through here?" Mark asked.

"Look closely at the big print. Then look at the smaller print. Which has more snow in them?"

"The big print," Paul said.

"You're right. Different snow means he came through earlier. How much snow did we get last night?" Jesse asked.

"Just a dusting," Mark answered.

"Right again. In order to have more than a dusting, the big guy must have come through before yesterday. Cole's print has just a dusting of snow in it. So he came through yesterday. You have to use everything you know when you look."

Dad, you said the big guy was hurt," Mark said.

"I think so. Focus only on the big prints. Try to ignore Cole's prints entirely. You have to focus to do it. Tell me if you notice anything."

Both boys stared at the tracks intently. Mark said, "I see it. I see a line in the snow. Every time the big guy takes a step with his right leg, there's a faint line, like he's dragging his right foot when he swings it forward."

Friends of the Family

"Very good, Mark. But there's something else. Look at the difference in the distance between the steps he takes with his left foot and his right foot. The big guy's definitely limping," Jesse said.

"Do you think Cole caught up with the man?" Paul asked deep in thought.

"He may have," Jesse said. "I don't know for sure. We need to talk about Cole anyway. You know that Cole has problems. There may or may not be something seriously wrong with Cole. But I don't believe for a minute Cole would ever hurt us. Do you?"

Both Mark and Paul shook their heads no.

"Neither does your mother. We think he's adopted our family in his own way. But I want to make this clear. If I ever think we're in danger from anyone, even Cole, I'll kill them like I would a mad dog."

"I understand, Dad," Paul said as he nodded his head solemnly.

"Good. I want us to work out some ground rules. Never ever leave the house without your weapon. If you encounter trouble, hide. If you can't hide, run. If you can't run, fight. And Paul, this fight has no rules," Jesse said. Paul nodded his head in understanding.

"Study how Cole stays out of sight. No more wandering down the middle of the street. Lastly, never ever let your mom or sister out of the house unless you or your brother's with them. We have a month, maybe two, before we leave. I want everyone in that truck when we pull out of here. So be smart. Adapt. These are hard times, and by God we're going to survive. Paul, it's time to grow up. I'm sorry, but it's got to be that way. Do you understand?" Jesse looked at his youngest son.

"I do," Paul answered.

"Good," Jesse smiled. "Now Paul, what would you like to do?"

"Follow the tracks," Paul said.

"You sure you want to find where they lead?" Jesse asked.

Paul stood and followed the tracks in the snow. Jesse and Mark trailed behind.

chapter 5

THE ONLY SNOW that remained outside Jesse's office was piled back under pine trees, in hard dirty hills encrusted with ice. Evenings in early April normally were in the forties, but tonight a warm breeze from the south remained. The fresh air smelled of the potential for spring and new growth.

Inside, Jesse and Paul stood and studied the truck. "This has to be the ugliest truck I've ever seen," Jesse said.

He walked up close to the truck and examined the camouflage paint job. Brown, green, and black intermixed in big blotches to simulate light and shade. The roof of the truck was a shooting blind. The shooter would have a full circle field of vision and from ten feet in the air. Jesse knew they were not going to outrun any anybody, but the truck would give them something to think about if they pursued them.

Jesse looked over as Cole and Mark came into the shop in a hurry. He could tell from the looks on their faces that something was wrong.

"Dad, we got a problem," Mark said.

"What?"

"The scavengers," Cole replied, "they're back."

"Are they the same ones as before?"

"Yeah and there are more of them. Lots more," Cole said.

"Where are they at right now?"

"They're camped out at the old Ferguson place this time. They got a real party going on."

"How long do you think we have before they come after Liberty?" Jesse asked.

"Two days, maybe less. We overheard some conversations. They're waiting for more people to show up in a day or two," Cole answered.

Jesse studied Mark and Cole. "Cole, go back and keep an eye on them and let us know if they make a move in this direction. Make sure you're back at the house by sundown. And for God's sake, make sure no one sees you."

Friends of the Family

"You got it," Cole answered over his shoulder as he headed out the door.

Jesse waited a few moments and then turned to his sons. "Guys, we're leaving first thing in the morning. Mark, I want you and Paul to visit anybody left in town and tell them that the scavengers are back and it looks like they're coming this way. They'll know what they have to do. Do not, I repeat, do not mention we are leaving. This is important. Nobody needs to know. Do you understand?"

Both boys nodded, grabbed their weapons and headed out the door. Jesse felt a rush of excitement. The waiting was over, he thought as he headed for Sarah. Jesse walked into the house and set his rifle in the corner of the living room. Sarah came down the stairs and stopped, looking at Jesse. "What's wrong?"

"The scavengers are back with reinforcements. Cole thinks we have a couple of days. I want us out of Liberty by day break tomorrow. I think we're ready, except for a few things I need to do to the truck."

"I think so too. We still have to pack, but not until dark. There's no sense announcing we are leaving."

By sunset they were ready. Jesse looked up as Mark and Paul came out of the house carrying their clothes they packed for the trip.

Cole came around the corner and walked up the drive and sat on the front step head down, looking at his hands in the gathering darkness.

"What's wrong?" Jesse asked.

"Nothing," Cole replied. "I just got a little too close. One of the scavengers almost spotted me and I had to lie low for awhile."

"What'd you find out?"

"We do have a couple of days. They are waiting for others to show up. But from what I could tell, they're definitely coming this way. That bunch's had a hard winter. Near as I could tell, most of them are sick with something."

Jesse walked over and sat on the step next to Cole. "Listen, Cole. We're leaving first thing in the morning. We want you to come with us." Jesse watched Cole study his dirty hands in the darkness for several moments. He notice tears in Cole's eyes.

"I know. I knew about the truck and figured you had a reason for all the secrets. Are you sure you want me with you, Mr. Colter?"

"Yes, son, we're sure. You're family now, Cole. We want you with us."

Cole looked back at his hands, a tear now running down his cheek. "Mr. Colter, I done things. Things I wish…"

Friends of the Family

"I know Cole. We all have. That's why we're leaving. We're going to find someplace where we can live in peace. Some place where we can all start over. But Cole, we're not there yet. We still got some tough work ahead of us. Do you understand what I mean?"

Cole stood up and looked down at Jesse.

"I understand, Mr. Colter. Now I'd like to go to the cemetery and say goodbye to my folks. I'll meet you at the garage in an hour with my things."

"That's a good idea, Cole," Jesse said as he stood up and shook Cole's hand.

"And Mr. Colter, I won't let anything bad happen to this family," Cole said looking Jesse in the eyes.

"I know, Cole, and neither will I."

Cole walked down the drive and headed in the direction of the cemetery. Jesse watched him go and turned back to his sons still standing on the front porch.

"Here we go, boys. Make sure you got your things together. We're going to pack the truck. I'll get your Mom and Lily."

When they reached the garage, there were two large duffel bags and four metal containers on the ground by the door. Jesse opened the top duffel bag. It was heavy and filled with weapons. The second bag was half full and contained mostly clothes. Laid on top of the clothes were some pictures of Cole's mother and father.

One of the pictures had been taken during the grand opening of a gas station. The picture showed a couple with a small boy of three or four, standing in front of the shiny new gas pumps. The woman smiled proudly up at the man. The man was grinning from ear to ear with self importance. The boy stood on the other side of the man, with one arm tightly gripping the man's leg. The little boy wasn't smiling at all.

Jesse zipped up the duffel bags and turned his attention to the metal army surplus ammo canisters. Each was filled with rounds of ammunition of various calibers. Two contained nothing but shotgun shells. Jesse carried the duffel bags into the staging area by the truck. The boys lugged the canisters inside.

Sarah climbed on a step and looked into the side door of the living area of the truck. She entered and sat on one of the four bunks attached to the walls. Jesse came over and stuck his head in the door.

"What do you think?" Jesse asked.

"It's a little claustrophobic at first," Sarah said, "but I think we'll get used to it. I hope we

Friends of the Family

don't have to spend twelve hours a day in this thing."

"We're going to be spending a lot of time inside, unless we're sure it's safe," Jesse replied. Sarah nodded as she climbed out of the middle area and took a walk around the truck examining the metal plates welded to the exterior.

"Where do you put the gas in, under the license plate?" Sarah asked a little sarcastically.

"Good one. Actually we have three fifty-gallon drums locked inside the back. Let me show you."

Sarah and Jesse clambered in through the back door, and stood in the storage area. "What are those other two drums?" Sarah asked.

"One's for kerosene and the other for water," Jesse answered. "Let me show you how we transfer fuel. I disconnected the outside filler tube, and rerouted it inside. It's right here by the drum of diesel fuel. See that hose running into the floor?"

Sarah nodded.

"That's how we transfer fuel into the truck's tank using the hand pump on the drum."

Both Sarah and Jesse stood in the door of the storage section of the truck and looked at the large pile of provisions sitting on the garage floor. Jesse climbed down and turned back to Sarah.

"You call out what you think we should take and the boys and I will get it for you. You stay up here and pack. Do you see the little door that connects the storage with the living area?"

Sarah glanced over at the opening and nodded her head.

"Good. Load the supplies you think we're most likely to need on the trip first. Anything we're taking all the way to Haven should be loaded last."

It was nearly midnight when they finished packing. They went through the stack one more time and closed the rear doors on the truck. Just as they were finishing, Cole arrived.

"Is that the last of it?" Jesse asked. Cole nodded yes.

"Everybody into the truck," Jesse said. "Mark, you ride shotgun." It struck Jesse s ironic that Mark really would be riding shotgun.

"Cole, once we head out, I'm going to need you up on the roof of the truck. You'll be riding up top most of the time. You should be able to keep an eye out for trouble from up there."

Friends of the Family

As Cole climbed in, Mark opened the large overhead door of the shop. Jesse took a final walk around the work area. He knew that this was the last time he would see this place. It was hard leaving.

Jesse climbed behind the wheel of the truck and turned the key. The diesel engine cranked and sprang into pounding life. The truck crept forward and out the big overhead door. Once on the street, Jesse dropped out of the cab and closed and carefully locked the big door of the garage. He knew there was little chance anyone would care if it was locked or not, he did it out of habit, one last reflection on his old way of life.

He drove home and the truck lumbered up their driveway. Everybody piled out and stood staring at the truck.

"Jesse, it's going to be a very long trip," Sarah said with obvious concern. "The living area is stuffy and loud, and those diesel fumes from the storage area are going to probably kill us. Lily almost passed out in back already and I have a headache."

"I'll see what I can do," Jesse replied. Maybe I can seal the little door with some duct tape. We'll trade places now and then up in the cab."

"Duct tape, I'm sure that will work," Sarah said under her breath as she headed towards the house.

Cole announced he would sleep up on the roof of the truck and Jesse was left with the impression that they might have to talk him down off of the roof once they got to Haven.

The dawn broke with the promise of rain. The warm southerly breeze remained. Everyone was a little grumpy as they climbed in the truck. Jesse and Sarah walked through the house one more time. Everything looked like the family was going to return in a week. As Jesse walked into the kitchen, he noticed the dishes neatly washed and stacked to dry.

They stood at the front door and looked around. Sarah cried softly and then disappeared back into the house sniffling, and returned with the embroidery piece that read *"God bless this home"* in an old fashioned picture frame.

"This goes wherever we go," Sarah said near tears, as she marched past Jesse to the truck and climbed in.

Jesse looked around one more time. He noticed the old grandfather clock in the corner had stopped at twelve o'clock and wondered if it had stopped at noon or midnight? Had it stop yesterday or a week ago? It was funny how time didn't really matter anymore. With a lump in his throat, Jesse closed the door and walked away.

chapter 6

Jesse headed the truck south out of Liberty. The road led directly to Utley, the next town over. Sarah and Jesse had studied the maps and laid out a route that circumvented main roads and cities. They were hoping to find a place where they could cross the Ohio River.

The old road now sprouted weeds through broken bits of asphalt, and Jesse noticed a small maple sapling pushing its way out of an especially nasty pothole. In spite of the road conditions, they were able to maintain a slow, but steady, speed most of the way to Utley. It had been months since Cole or Jesse had made it this far from Liberty. They approached the outskirts of the town and Jesse stopped on a hill overlooking the village. Sarah stuck her head out of the back area into the cab.

"Are we there yet, Daddy?" Sarah said in her best Betty Boop voice.

"That's not funny, Sarah. Look at this place."

The town of Utley was a shambles. It had been burnt to the ground. The high school was now four brick walls surrounding a vast pile of rubble where the roof collapsed. The other structures in the town were piles of charred boards and ashes. Jesse drove slowly and stopped only to make sure that rubble in the road didn't puncture the truck tires.

They proceeded southeast towards Middletown. About half way there, Jesse again stopped. Three cars blocked the road. One was upside down, the other two locked together in the embrace of the crash. A wooded area was close on the left side of the road. Paul's head popped through the opening this time.

"Get your Mom," Jesse said to him. Sarah's head appeared through the window behind the front seat..

"Come up and drive. I'm going to walk down through the woods on the left and make sure this is what it appears to be."

"Good. It's time for a break anyway," Sarah said.

Friends of the Family

Jesse climbed out of the cab, dragged his shotgun out from behind the seat, and disappeared into the trees. Sarah got into the cab and waited.

After several minutes, Jesse appeared from the trees by the wreck on the side of the road. He climbed on top of the overturned car, and motioned for Sarah to pull forward. As the truck approached, Jesse jumped down and stood by the side of the road. Sarah pulled to a stop. Jesse saw Cole on the roof of the truck rise up and study the tree line through his scope. Jesse walked up to the driver's window.

"Put the truck in creeper gear and gently push the car on its top off the road. This was a bad wreck. What's left of a body is still in the overturned car. Be gentle. I don't want to hurt the truck."

Sarah nodded and looked intently at the gearshift as she searched for the creeper position. It ground a little as she engaged it. Easing out the clutch, the truck crept forward. The overturned car protested with a high-pitched screech as the truck nudged the car across the asphalt and onto the shoulder of the road. Once they cleared the wreck site Sarah opened the driver's door. Jesse ran up.

"No Sarah, you drive. You can drive this thing as well as I can. I'll ride in back for awhile."

"No problem," Sarah said. "I wouldn't mind breathing something besides diesel fumes for a while."

Jesse climbed into the back as Sarah eased the truck forward. For much of the six miles to Middletown, Jesse kept popping his head through the window to see what was going on. "You're driving me crazy. Sit back and relax. I'll yell if I see anything," Sarah finally told him.

"Okay, but stop before you get into Middletown proper," Jesse said as he pulled his head back.

Sarah pulled to a stop as the truck rounded the last curve before entering the town. She and Jesse traded places. Jesse drove slowly past the outskirts.

The houses appeared recently abandoned but at least were still standing. Trash was everywhere. It looked like someone had systematically ransacked the homes. Windows were broken, and curtains fluttered silently from the gapping frames. Somewhere a screen door banged. No smoke rose from the houses.

Friends of the Family

Someone's ugly green sofa sat in the middle of the main street. Jesse pulled into a gas station after several blocks and stopped.

"It's almost noon, Sarah. I think we should rest a while. How about some lunch?" Jesse asked.

"How far have we come?" Paul asked.

"Well it was twelve miles to Utley, and another fourteen miles to Middletown. So we've made about twenty five miles. We're about eight miles from the interstate, and I want to be well clear of that place by dark. We should leave in about an hour or so," Jesse said.

Cole threw down the rope ladder from the top of the truck and joined everyone else. Sarah passed out sandwiches and glasses of water mixed with Tang. Lily appeared to Jesse to be a little green around the gills, but began to recover nicely once she was out of the truck.

As soon as Cole was finished eating, he went back to the truck's roof and resumed his vigil. Suddenly, Jesse saw Cole tense, pointing back towards town. At the same time he heard a noise he couldn't place.

"Everybody, back in the truck," Jesse said. He grabbed his shotgun, ran to the building next to gas station, and waited. The noise began as a nest of angry hornets. As it grew in volume, it sounded to Jesse like a bunch of chain saws. Then it hit him, motorcycles!

As he peeked around the corner of the building, three motorcycles came around the curve of the road. The lead cycle held a single rider. The other two cycles carried two passengers, two men on one, and a man and girl on the other. The three cycles roared to a stop next to the sofa in the middle of the street. They revved their engines and shut them off.

The men climbed off the cycles. It was hard to tell from three blocks away, but Jesse thought the girl's hands were tied behind her to the upright on the back of the seat. She was definitely gagged.

The men were standing in a circle around the girl. They were laughing and passing a bottle around. The girl had no coat; her thin dress afforded her little protection from the cold. Her dress was pulled up exposing white thighs. She looked terrified, even from this distance.

Jesse crouched and ran back to the truck.

"Cole, come down," Jesse whispered. "Mark, get your shotgun. The rest of you lock the doors and stay quiet."

Friends of the Family

The boys crouched down by Jesse. Both looked concerned, their eyes round with attention.

"It looks like we've got some scavengers."

They nodded their heads.

"We can't get across the street, so we need to watch our line of fire."

Jesse drew a quick map with his finger in the dirt.

"Cole, you get to this point here. Do *not* fire until I do. Mark you go with me. When I point, you stay. Make sure they don't see you. I counted four bad guys. I'll take out the big guy with the first shot. Mark, you try for the one with the leather vest. Cole, you and I will clean up the other two. Got it?"

Jesse looked at the boys. They both nodded again.

"We'll give Cole three minutes to get to his position. Now move."

The three minutes seemed to drag on forever. Jesse went back to the corner of the building and watched the bikers. The big one now straddled the bike facing the girl. He reached out and ripped the front of the girl's dress to her waist. She struggled and appeared to be weeping uncontrollably. The big one began pawing her.

Jesse crouched and ran back to where Mark waited. "Let's go."

Jesse and Mark ran, pausing as they passed areas that opened to the street with the sofa. Finally they drew even with the bikers and the girl. The bikers were laughing and bragging about what they were going to do to the girl.

The one with the vest began to untie her hands. Jesse pointed to some steel drums for Mark to hide behind and moved on to the other side of the alley for a clear view of what was going on. He estimated he was thirty feet from the sofa. The girl was now on the ground as they struggled to get her dress off. She was putting up a good fight.

"God damn you losers! I got to do everything," the big one yelled as he walked over to where the girl struggled. He made a fist and hit her on the side of the head. The girl shuddered once and lay still.

Jesse's shot exploded like a thunderclap lifting the big one four feet into the air and opened a red bloom in the middle of his chest. The other three froze in surprise. Mark's blast came from Jesse's left. The vested biker was cut down at the knees and fell to the ground screaming. The remaining two dove for the sofa for cover. The girl rolled over and moaned.

Seconds ticked by. *Where's Cole?* Jesse wondered. The two behind the sofa drew hand guns and shot wildly in Jesse and Mark's direction. Jesse saw the dazed girl sit up and then stand. Blood ran down the side of her head to her chin. Slowly she stumbled towards the sofa.

One of the bikers behind the sofa stood and shot her in the chest point blank. The crack of a high-powered rifle sounded as the shooter's head exploded, sending a fine spray of blood into the air.

The vested biker continued to roll around on the ground, screaming in pain at the loss of his knees. The fourth biker apparently lost his nerve, and broke for the other side of the street. As Cole's bullet entered his back, it shattered his spine and he dropped like a sack of dirt.

He lay in the street, his low moans complementing the screams of the vested guy with no knees. Jesse pumped another shell into the chamber and stepped out from the shadows. Mark emerged behind him.

"Jesus…oh Jesus, help me man." No Knees was sobbing.

Jesse pointed his shotgun, holding it with one hand. He pulled the trigger and the vested biker lay still. He pumped the shotgun, chambering another shell. He walked over to the one moaning from the spine shot and pulled the trigger again. Mark walked to where the girl lay crumpled on the ground. He covered her with what was left of her dress. Jesse pushed the cycles into a heap, opened the gas caps, and lit a match. The cycles lit up with a WHUMP.

"Just in case they have friend. Let's go Mark," Jesse said. He and Mark walked slowly down the street towards the truck. Cole was waiting for them.

"Okay everybody, you can come on out now. It's over," Jesse said.

Sarah opened the door, stepped out, and gave Jesse a hug.

"I think we better move on," Jesse said. "We don't want to be here if their friends show up."

Cole and Mark climbed up on the roof in a hurry, as everyone else piled into the truck. Jesse eased out of the station heading towards the interstate. He glanced in the rearview mirror and saw smoke rising from the charred remains of the motorcycles as they passed the city limits.

Friends of the Family

They drove on through most of the afternoon and saw no sign of life anywhere. As they drew closer to the interstate, the number of abandoned cars rose rapidly. Jesse drove by a sign that read 'I-75, one mile'.

As he cleared a rise in the road, cars and trucks were scattered everywhere. Some had bullet-riddled windshields, but most appeared as if they were abandoned when they ran out of gas. Jesse stopped. Sarah stuck her head through the hole in the cab.

"I think we're going to have to backtrack," Jesse said. "I don't see any way through this mess. It looks like a parking lot for the insane. I'm pretty sure I saw a small paved road about a mile back that might get us out of here".

Jesse horsed the truck around backtracking to the small road. It headed off in a northerly direction. Trees canopied the road, and weeds and shrubs crowded the brim. Jesse kept his speed down as he rounded the twisting curves. After a mile the road ended at an unmarked intersection. Jesse turned right and headed east again.

The second road was as narrow as the first. After another mile the pavement ended abruptly. The dry and powdery dirt bellowed out behind the truck. The road appeared to narrow even further. Limbs from trees and bushes on both sides of the road scraped the sides of the truck.

The ruts in the road forced Jesse to slow even more. They bounced and jarred for about another half a mile. The truck made a sharp turn and rolled down a steep hill into a small secluded valley where Jesse stopped. On each side of the road, lay a grassy meadow. The grass was a deep and vibrant green with little yellow flowers dotting it.

Jesse walked to where a brook ran through the meadow on the right. The water was so clear, Jesse could see spawn beds on the bottom. Rocks broke the surface, and the setting sun's light, forced Jesse to close his eyes. He heard a soft breeze high up in the trees. Sarah, Lily and Paul clambered out of the truck and joined Jesse. A dusty, scratched Cole and Mark joined them as they stared at the valley that lay before them.

"Cole, Mark, you guys check your weapons and take a walk up this road for half an hour or so. Then head back. That should be about two miles. Keep to the sides of the road. Let us know if you see anything," Jesse said.

The boys headed off, Cole on one side and Mark on the other. They disappeared quickly at the top of hill. "Jesse this valley is gorgeous," Sarah exclaimed.

Friends of the Family

"It couldn't have come along at a better time. Let's spend the night here. I think we could all use a good night's rest."

Paul and Lilly headed down to the brook to wash up and Jesse could hear water splashing a short time later. Sarah unloaded food from the truck and Jesse returned with an armload of wood.

"Do you think we should risk a fire, Jesse?"

"The breeze up in those trees should disperse the smoke, but I'll wait for the all-clear from the boys before I light it. After Middletown, I think we need a fire just to lift our spirits."

"What happened?" Sarah asked.

"Some bikers rode in with a girl tied to the back of their bikes. They were just starting in on her when we surprised them. It was bad."

"What about the girl?"

"One of the bikers took her out," Jesse said. He looked at Sarah, shook his head and then tried to look busy laying out the campfire on the edge of the meadow.

A short time later, Cole and Mark returned. "Everything's cool, Dad," Mark said. "We went a little further because the road changed back into a paved road about a mile ahead. We didn't see anything. Not even a house or a mailbox."

Joel Baker

After they finished eating, the boys and Lily went down by the stream and washed up. Even Cole joined them quietly at the edge of the group. Night came quickly to the valley. Once they were ready for bed, they sat around the campfire and studied the burning embers. After awhile Cole climbed up top. Mark and Paul helped their little sister into the truck.

Sarah went in to check on them. She came out with a towel, shampoo, and soap. "Would you mind terribly, sir, accompanying me down by the water?" Sarah asked in her best southern drawl.

"Why certainly, Mrs. Colter," Jesse answered. "And I would like to assure you that I will avert my eyes at all times to respect your privacy."

"Yeah, right," Sarah answered with a laugh as they walked down to the brook and found a small pool formed behind some rocks. Sarah slowly disrobed, and knelt by the still pool washing her hair. Jesse sat on the grassy edge of the pool, enjoying the moment, but thinking about what lay ahead.

chapter 7

DAWN CAME LATE to the small valley. By the time the sun worked its way over the hills, everything was packed and loaded. Jesse wanted to get as far away as possible from Middletown. The truck started hard, but after a few tries, the engine coughed to life and the loaded truck lumbered up the hill and out of the valley.

The pavement returned about a mile up the road just as the boys had said. The ruts in the shoulder of the road forced Jesse to drive down the center. They were still headed east when they came to a four-way stop sign. Jesse turned right, south towards the Ohio River.

An hour later they entered Moss. It appeared to be the typical southern Ohio small town. A bit dumpy on the outskirts, the houses improved steadily as they approached the business district surrounding the town square.

Jesse drove slowly past empty two-story buildings, an Ace hardware store, the First Ohio Bank, an occasional bar, and a diner.

Sarah pointed out the Church of God and the Church of God Reformed that sat next to each other. Apparently there'd been some fundamental disagreement between the two churches in the past. There must have been some awkward Sunday mornings.

A mile outside town Jesse spotted what appeared to be a small roadside park. Trash was scattered on the ground. Jesse pulled in and stopped. He and Sarah climbed out and surveyed the area.

"This is nasty," Sarah said, wrinkling her nose. "Paul, Lilly, come on out and let's pick this place up." Paul and Lily jumped out the side door and began picking up the trash gingerly and placing it in a pile.

"Couldn't you have found a better place to stop than this?" Sarah asked.

"Probably," Jesse replied. "But I don't like pulling the truck off the road just anywhere and maybe getting stuck. By the way, did you notice anything about that little town we just drove through?"

"It was nice enough. It kind of reminded me of Liberty, but no, I didn't see anything special. Why?" Sarah asked.

"It just struck me that it was the first town we've driven through that only had a few broken windows and no burned buildings, that sort of thing."

"What do you think it means?"

"I'm not sure. Maybe we're getting close to civilization. Apparently scavengers haven't been through here. There must be a reason." Jesse looked around. "Where's Cole?"

"I don't know. Mark, have you seen Cole?"

Mark pointed towards the rise running next to the park. "He went up there."

"Just great," Jesse said, walking back to the cab and getting a rifle. "I'll go look for him."

"I'll fix us some lunch," Sarah said.

Jesse climbed over the fence and to the top of the small hill behind the roadside park. He could see Cole behind some trees at the top of the next ridge.

He walked over to where Cole stood staring intently at something beyond the row of trees.

"What's going on?" Jesse asked quietly.

"There's a house down there, and I thought I heard a faint voice calling for help. I think it's coming from the house."

"Did you see anything?"

"No, it looks all closed up, but I think someone is in there. Three dogs are roaming around the place. They seem to be after something inside."

"Let's take a look," Jesse said, heading back to the trees. He watched for a few minutes as several large dogs kept walking up on the porch of the house, sniffing at the door, and then walking off.

"Cole, the people in that house are probably dead. We've seen this before."

"I know, but I really think I heard a voice from down there."

Jesse thought about it for a minute. Cole had an instinct for these situations. "That's good enough for me. I wsant you to go back and tell Mark and Mrs. Colter what's going on. Then Bring Mark back with you and your weapons. Tell Paul to get up on the roof of the truck with his rifle and stay alert. I'll wait here."

After Cole headed back, Jesse watched the house for any sign of life. He thought he might have seen a ghostly shadow move past one of the windows. A fourth dog appeared from behind the house just after Mark and Cole returned with high-powered rifles with scopes.

"We're going to take those dogs out," Jesse said. "Mark you take the big yellow one out front. I'll take the smaller brown one on the right. Cole, you take the big brown on the porch. Set your scopes for a hundred yards."

"What about the fourth one?" Cole asked.

"Take him out if you can, but he'll probably be moving fast."

The boys spread out ten yards on each side of Jesse. When they were in position and sighted, Jesse placed the crosshairs on the smaller dog on the right.

The barrel of his rifle jerked up as he fired. The sound of Mark and Cole's shots followed closely. Then a final *crack*, as Cole went for the fourth dog. Jesse saw his dog on its side, dead in the dirt.

"Did you get the fourth dog?" Jesse asked Cole.

"I hit it. I saw him do a cartwheel in the air. He was really moving though, so I'm not sure it was a clean kill."

"Let's take a walk down to the house," Jesse said, "but be really careful, and keep your spacing."

All three headed down the rise, out of the trees, and towards the house. Cole pointed, and Jesse could see the fourth dog dead in the weeds. They walked up in front of the porch and stopped. Jesse thought he heard a baby crying.

"Hello! Is anybody in there?" Jesse called. This time Jesse definitely saw a curtain move.

A woman's voice called from the house. "Is it safe to come out? Are the dogs dead?"

"It's safe," Jesse called back.

The door opened and a frightened young woman walked out holding a baby. She was followed by a little boy, who looked to be three years old. The woman appeared to be in her late twenties, but It was difficult to tell because of the dirt. Her mousy brown hair was thin and scraggly. Jesse thought she and her children were showing the first signs of malnutrition.

"Oh, thank God you came by," the woman said, looking both frightened and relieved at the same time. "We've been trapped in here for three days by those damn dogs." The little boy peeked out at Jesse from behind his mother's dress.

"Glad to help," Jesse said. "Is there just the three of you?"

"Yes. We ran low on food, and my husband went to see if he could get some from Fairfax. He headed out almost a week ago," the woman said, obviously concerned. "You haven't seen him, have you?"

Friends of the Family

"Sorry, we haven't seen anyone. Mark, head back and have your mother bring the truck up. It looks like this access road runs out to the main road."

"It does," the woman volunteered.

Mark headed back toward the trees and Jesse walked up on the porch. "I'm Jesse Colter. This is Cole."

"Please to meet you. My name's Nancy Porter and this is my son Justin," the woman said shaking Jesse's hand. "You wouldn't have any food to spare, would you? My children need food badly."

"We'll see what we can do. Mrs. Porter, how far is this Fairfax place?"

"Call me Nancy. It's a town about ten miles south from here. Ernie, my husband, knew there were people there, so he thought he could get us some help."

Jesse looked back as the truck lumbered down the path and up to the house. An hour later, the dogs were dragged into the brush and Sarah had everyone fed.

She'd cleaned up Justin and the house as best she could while Nancy was inside feeding the baby. Sarah walked out on the porch and sat on the front steps by Jesse.

"Is there something wrong Jesse?" Sarah asked, seeing that Jesse appeared angry.

"I'm just ticked off that her husband would go off like that and leave his wife and kids unprotected like this."

"He must have thought they were safe here and..."

"Well, thoughts like that can get you killed."

"What do you think we should do with Nancy and her children? We can't leave them here," Sarah said.

"I checked the map and Fairfax is in the direction we're heading. We can't leave them here. I guess we'll take them to Fairfax, and hope her husband made it."

"You think he did?"

"Not really. He's been gone almost a week. It should have taken him a half of day there, and a half a day back."

"Will the folks in Fairfax look after them?"

"...if there are people in Fairfax," Jesse said.

"Let's stay here tonight. It would be nice to have a roof over our head."

"It can't hurt," Jesse replied, almost smiling. "We can leave in the morning. It's too late to start this afternoon anyway."

Jesse's attitude improved by morning. With everyone washed and fed, they loaded the truck. The three boys climbed up top, while

Friends of the Family

Nancy with the baby Elisabeth went in back. Lily was already there entertaining Justin with her stuffed toys. Jesse looked over at Sarah, shook his head, and drove out to the road and headed south towards Fairfax.

The morning was uneventful. After about ten miles, they began to see smoke coming from chimneys. Occasionally someone would come out on a porch and stare at the truck as if it were a mirage. Jesse and Sarah saw this as a sign of approaching civilization.

Jesse grew more confident and tried to keep his speed up. They were close to the Ohio River and the terrain was surprisingly hilly. Nothing like what's ahead, Jesse thought, but lots of hills just the same. Finally they passed a sign indicating they were coming to Fairfax. As Jesse rounded a curve, he stopped the truck in front of a barricade extending across the road.

"We must be here," Jesse announced.

Several rifles appeared over the rampart and a voice called out. "Better shut her down buddy. That's as far as you go!"

Jesse shut off the engine. He opened the cab door and stood in the door of the truck making sure that his hands could be seen.

Jesse smiled towards the voice. "Easy fella. Just my family and me passing through."

"Where you headed?" The voice asked.

"Tennessee. We're looking for a bridge across the Ohio that's still standing," Jesse answered.

"Where'd ya think you would cross?" the voice said.

"Well, I thought Ripley. Have you ever heard of it?"

"Yep. Got a brother from Ripley. How'd you know about the bridge? It ain't on any map," the voice asked.

"My wife and I were planning this trip, and we thought that the marked bridges would be blocked or in the water," Jesse said, keeping a close watch on the barricade. "So I spotted Ripley, Ohio on the map and South Ripley, Kentucky across the river. I said to my wife, who would be crazy enough to name towns like that and not have a bridge between them? So I figured we'd go down and take a look to see if they had a bridge or if they really were that crazy."

An old man's head appeared over the barricade. He laid a shotgun on top an engine hood of an old Pontiac. He took off a straw hat and wiped his brow with his shirt sleeve.

Jesse continued to smile at the man. The old man put his hat back on and looked towards Jesse for a minute.

Friends of the Family

"Well, I got my brother right here, and he just told me he saw the bridge when he left and it was standing. How much that truck weigh?" the old man asked.

"Near as I can tell loaded, about six ton," Jesse answered.

The old man laughed. "Hope you feel lucky, cause that's a five ton bridge. Where'd you come from?"

"Little town up toward Dayton called Liberty."

"Never heard of it. Of course there's lots of places I ain't heard of. You come through Middletown?" the old man asked.

"Believe we did. Sorry place it was too," Jesse answered.

"You happen to see some bikers up that way?" the old man asked.

"Now that you mention it, we did."

"Mean bastards, weren't they?"

"Not anymore," Jesse said.

The old man thought for a second, then bent down to say something to one of the people behind the barricade.

"How many in your family?" the old man asked.

"My wife, daughter, and three boys," Jesse answered. "We also got a family that lives around here with us. Their name's Porter. Have you seen anything of a guy named Ernie Porter? He was heading this way looking for help for his family."

"Yeah, he's here. He dragged in, day before yesterday, in bad shape. He kept trying to tell us something, but we couldn't understand him. He must have been telling us about his family."

"Well, his wife and kids will be glad to hear he's alive. Any chance we can drop off his family and pass on through?"

The old man leaned over and said something else to those behind the barricades. There appeared to be some sort of heated argument.

"You can drop off the Porters," the old man said. "We take care of our own. But I'm afraid you all will have to keep moving. It ain't nothing personal."

"Not a problem," Jesse answered. "If your brother's here, would you ask him if we should expect trouble in Ripley?"

More visiting took place between the old man and the others behind the barricade. "Not anymore," the old man answered.

Jesse watched as several men and boys began clearing the road. "They're going to let us through," Jesse said, climbing back in the truck and moving forward. "Keep your heads down."

The truck eased past the barricade. They stopped long enough to let the Porters out and then rolled through the little town that appeared armed to the teeth. As they approached the far side of town, a space was cleared to let the truck exit. Most of the men in town stood and watched as Jesse headed the truck for Ripley and the Ohio River.

chapter 8

JESSE AND SARAH decided they didn't want to be on the road after dark. They found a garage big enough to hold the truck in the next town. Jesse backed in and shut it down. That night rain came and when they awoke in the morning, it was still drizzling.

The family ate a quick breakfast as Sarah broke out the powdered milk for the kids and coffee for her and Jesse. After breakfast Mark crawled into the storage area and transferred fuel from the barrel into the fuel tank.

The rain concerned Jesse. If their heavy truck were to go off the pavement it could easily get stuck in soft dirt or mud. Nobody wanted to walk from here. They pulled out of the garage and continued on the road south, until they came to a dead end at a two lane highway. Jesse pulled out the maps and found their location.

The highway ran from Cincinnati, along the Ohio River, in a southeasterly direction through Ripley. He hoped the bridge was still intact and open. Sarah and he were certain that major bridges around big cities would be blocked and impassable.

As they neared Ripley, the highway narrowed to a single lane because of all the abandoned cars on both shoulders of the road. Jesse weaved back and forth to avoid them.

He had to push several into the ditch. Most hoods were up and white rags were tied to the antennas in case help in the form of a tow truck showed up. The cars appeared to have been there for some time.

It was slow going but just before noon they stopped on the top of a hill overlooking Ripley. The bridge sat in full view at the bottom, still intact. Two cars, facing nose-to-nose, blocked the entrance.

Houses ran down the left side of the road facing the river. A bridge spanned the river at its narrowest point. Several concrete pilings supported the structure. Jesse could see the road on the other side of the river. It was tree lined, unblocked, and appeared relatively

Friends of the Family

open. The highway they were on continued for some ways beyond the bridge entrance and disappeared around a curve.

Jesse backed the truck off the crest of the hill, and shut it down. He climbed out of the cab, picked up his shotgun, and walked around to the other side as the truck door opened. Sarah and the kids climbed out.

"I'm going to take a walk closer to the bridge, and check out the houses overlooking the bridge entrance. I should be back in an hour or so. Please, everybody, no wandering off," Jesse said.

He looked up at the roof of the truck. "Cole, stay alert."

Jesse headed off into the field on the side of the road and lost sight of the truck. He approached the first house and it looked like it was occupied. He dropped down and eased around the garage away from the house. Smoke was rising from the chimney and clothes hung limply on the line running from the garage to the house in spite of the clouds and drizzle.

After a few minutes, a boy of about twelve came out of the back door and headed for the house next door carrying a fishing pole. He walked up to the back door and knocked. A woman came to the door wearing a ragged pink bathrobe that exposed a little too much. Jesse was close enough to hear their voices.

"What do you want?" the woman asked.

"Is Jeffery home?" the boy asked.

"Nope. He went with his Daddy and uncles to check out some folks that moved into the old Langley place up the highway. They should be back in a couple of hours. You want me to tell Jeffery you stopped by?" the woman asked.

"Yeah. Tell him I want to go fishing or something. Thanks." The boy headed back towards his house and went back inside with a slam of the wooden screen door. The woman looked around for a bit and then disappeared back into her house.

Jesse crouched and backed out the way he came. Sarah and the kids were standing outside the truck when he returned.

"I say we try it now," Jesse said. "It appears as though most of the men have gone somewhere and won't be back for a couple of hours. This may be our best time to try the crossing. What do you think Sarah?"

"I think we have to try now. Kids, get back in the truck."

Jesse climbed up in the cab and started the engine. "Hang on everyone. I'm going to have to push those cars blocking the bridge out of the way. Everybody say a prayer and think light thoughts, we're a ton over the bridge weight limit."

The truck broke the crest of the hill and headed down towards the cars at the entrance to the bridge. As they got closer, Jesse slowed somewhat and downshifted from third to second to first. When he pulled up to the cars, Jesse plowed forward, shoving the first car into the second. The two cars kissed and both cars slid to the railing on the far side of the bridge entrance with the sound of screeching metal.

As Jesse slammed the gearshift into reverse he noticed the boy he'd watched earlier run out onto the front porch. A minute later, Mrs. Bathrobe emerged onto her front steps as well. Several other people came out of a house further down the street, and three men started walking, then running towards the bridge entrance.

Jesse slammed on the brakes. He fought the steering wheel into a hard right and crawled out onto the bridge. Jesse strangled the steering wheel with white knuckles as the truck rolled forward. He knew they had about six inches on either side of the truck. Slowly they gained speed. The bridge groaned. Jesse glanced in the rearview mirror. The three men ran out onto the bridge and after the truck. When the bridge protested, the men pulled up short, and ran with legs pumping, back the way they came.

Not a good sign, Jesse thought.

"Ahhhh, Dad? If we're going in the river, a little speed isn't going to matter. Can you speed it up a little?" Mark asked.

Jesse floored the accelerator. Now both the bridge and the truck protested. Jesse slammed the truck into third and began to pick up more speed.

As the Kentucky side drew nearer, the bridge complained loudly. Jesse pounded the steering wheel in frustration. When the truck reached the Kentucky end of the bridge, the front end of the truck dropped hard on the bridge exit.

Jesse hit the brakes as hard as he could. The truck swerved and skidded to a halt up against the grassy bank of the far side of the road. Jesse cranked the steering wheel hard right, pulled away from the bank, and headed west down a highway on the Kentucky side of the Ohio River.

Sarah stuck her head into the cab. A few hundred feet from the bridge was a road to the left with a sign which read 'South Ripley, two miles' with an arrow pointing up the road. Jesse plunged forward past the turnoff.

"I've had enough of Ripley for one day," Jesse commented.

"Gee, that was fun. Would you like for me to drive for a while?" Sarah asked.

Jesse looked back in his rearview mirror towards the bridge entrance. He saw four men mounted on horses come galloping up to the three men standing by the bridge entrance. The one on the lead horse jumped down and appeared to be exchanging words with the three standing men. The one holding the horse's lead was animated as he took off his hat and threw it to the ground.

"I'll drive for now. It looks like the posse's arrived, and they're not happy about us using their bridge. And I'm serious about the posse, four guys on horseback. We've got to get off this highway. Sarah? Got any ideas?" Jesse asked.

"According to the map, there's a little road about a mile on up. It looks like it heads due south, but with no towns. The road looks like it heads nowhere."

"Sounds perfect," Jesse said, slowing when he saw the entrance to the road on the left. About half a mile down the road and around a curve, Jesse stopped and shut the engine off.

He opened the door of the cab, and used the window as a step up to the roof of the truck. Jesse listened carefully. All he could hear was the occasional ting of raindrops striking the metal top of the truck. Jesse listened for a few minutes and heard nothing but the rain. He looked at the lumpy tarp and the two eyes peering out from under it.

"Cole, walk back up the road a couple of hundred yards or so and make sure we're not being followed. If they follow us, shoot the horses. They can't chase us on foot."

Cole climbed down and headed back up the road, just as the doors of the truck opened and everybody climbed out.

"Daddy, we need seatbelts," Lily said. "Cause we kept bouncing all over the place and Mommy said a bad word."

"We'll see what we can do Lily," Jesse said. "What bad word did Mommy say?"

"Never mind," Sarah said. "Lily? Let's you and me go for a walk." As she and Lily left, Sarah stuck her tongue out at Jesse.

Something bothered Jesse other than they were being chased by men on horseback. He had a spooky feeling something wasn't quite

Friends of the Family

right. After Sarah and Lily returned, it came to him.

"Sarah, let me see the map. Mark, did you see the name of this road when we turned on it?"

"It didn't have a sign. I looked," Mark said.

"You go back up the road to Cole and take your rifle."

As Mark headed out, Jesse took the map from Sarah and they both studied it sitting on the running board of the truck. He found Ripley, South Ripley, and the road they were on. It followed a serpentine path in a southwest direction.

"This road must be over a hundred miles long. It ends about twenty miles from the Tennessee border. There's not a single town on it, yet the town of Ripley with its eight or ten houses is clearly marked. This is very, very odd," Jesse said, thinking out loud.

But something else bothered Jesse. It's what had made him curious in the first place. "Sarah, the road's made of pure concrete with wide gravel shoulders. This takes lots of money. Only the federal government builds roads like this. But why build it here?"

A short time later, Cole and Mark walked up to where Jesse sat deep in thought staring at the map, and squatted down beside him and waited. After a while Jesse looked up at them.

"Well?" Jesse asked a worried look on his face.

"Dad, it was kind of creepy," Mark said. "I got next to Cole just as the four guys on horses went thundering by the turnoff for this road. About five minutes later they came back and stopped. The leader said something to the other three, and headed up the road towards us."

Mark bit his lip before continuing. "The other three never moved a lick, just sat on their horses staring. The leader pulled up and went back to the other three, and everybody started yelling at each other and waving their arms. We couldn't make out what they were saying, but you know what I think?"

"What?"

"I don't think those other three guys wanted anything to do with this road. Nothing could get them to ride this way. They looked kind of, I don't know, spooked." Cole nodded his agreement.

"We're on a road to nowhere. The locals are scared to go down it...but not too frightened to chase an obviously well-armed truck on horseback. What do they know?" Jesse asked, not expecting an answer.

He got up and walked to the front of the truck and leaned against the grill. Sarah followed. Jesse looked down the long expanse of perfect road that lay like a white ribbon in front of them.

Suddenly the hairs on the back of his neck stood up. It felt like there was someone or something out there, like they were being watched. He looked back over his shoulder and Cole was in a crouch looking around, his gun at the ready as well.

"Someone's watching us. I don't think I'm imagining things, Sarah. Cole feels it too. Let's get the hell out of here," Jesse said. He and Sarah ran for the truck.

"We've got another hour or two of daylight and an open road. Sarah you drive. I'm going up on the roof with Cole. Mark, you ride shotgun. Let's go, people."

chapter 9

THE WHITE CONCRETE road continued through heavily wooded hills. At various points, red limestone cliffs standing thirty to forty feet high lined both sides of the road. Sarah began to pick up speed. Jesse still had a weird feeling about what lay ahead. He leaned over the front corner of the cab and told her to slow up.

"Cole, do you still feel it too?" Jesse asked, after another ten miles. Cole nodded.

As evening approached, a blue line crossed the sky as it began to clear. The sun finally appeared and then disappeared with evening. Sarah flashed on the truck lights and kept moving. After another hour, she stopped. She climbed out the cab into the darkness and stretched. Jesse used the rope ladder and joined her on the ground. She looked worried.

"What's wrong?" Jesse asked.

"I don't know," Sarah replied. "It's just that, well, it's all too easy. Where are the wrecks? Where are the abandoned cars? Here's a road that heads due south, and yet it doesn't appear to have been used by anyone. No houses, no towns, I don't know why, but I've got a feeling..."

"Cole and I feel it too. It's like we're being watched. Plus, this road just doesn't belong here. Something isn't right."

"We can't go back, Jesse, and we're making good time."

"Alright, but everyone sleeps in the truck. Mark and Cole will take turns keeping watch tonight."

The night sky continued to clear and was sprinkled with stars. The temperature dropped and Sarah emerged from the truck with three coats. She handed them to Jesse, Mark, and Cole. The coats were handmade of heavy six-ounce tent canvas and were a light brown color. Jesse put on the stiff coat. It fit well, reaching almost to the top of his boots.

"The coat's great, Sarah. It's like wearing your own tent," Jesse commented.

"Exactly," Sarah replied. "It should keep you warm and dry. I copied the pattern out of an old catalog. The split up the back is called a saddle break. It's for riding a horse, I think. Did you see all the pockets on the inside?"

Both boys tried their coats on. They were too large, but Sarah said they'd grow into them. Mark took the first watch and woke Cole a little after midnight. It was definitely cold and Cole could see his breath as he took up his rifle. About three hours later Cole leaned over by the driver's side window and gently knocked on the window. Jesse came awake with a jolt, and climbed up to the roof of the truck.

"Did you see anything?" Jesse asked, rubbing his eyes to wake up.

"No. Thought I saw some tree limbs move, but I'm not sure," Cole replied. He went and laid down covering himself with a tarp.

Jesse sat and looked long and hard, but decided it was too dark to really see anything. Once it became light, Jesse could hear stirrings in the cab below. Pretty soon Sarah and Lily came out, heading towards the woods.

"Don't go too far," Jesse cautioned.

They came back in a few minutes at a dead run. Jesse jumped to his feet and scanned the woods behind them. Sarah and Lily came to a breathless stop by the truck right beneath where Jesse stood.

"What's wrong?" Jesse asked.

"I don't know for sure," Sarah said obviously shaken, "All I know is that there's something big and black out there. I saw a shadow moving. We just ran and never looked back. Let's get out of here. I do not like it."

Everyone piled in and Jesse fired the up the truck. They headed south and after five or six more miles of unbroken wilderness, Jesse pulled slowly to a stop. About a hundred yards ahead, off to the right, was a white concrete driveway leading into the woods.

Jesse climbed out of the truck and Sarah came up to the driver's seat. Jesse told her to keep the engine going while they checked out the driveway. He and Mark came around the truck and waved for Cole to join them.

"We need to check this out. It's the first sign of life since we got on this road. I'll go first. Mark you follow me by about twenty feet. Cole you take the rear about twenty feet behind Mark. Maintain your spacing. If something comes down, don't shoot each other or me. Keep to the sides." Both boys nodded. The three figures in long brown coats headed into the driveway and disappeared into the woods.

Friends of the Family

    Jesse constantly checked the woods beside them. The sunlight filtered through the branches of the trees on either side. It got muggy in the deep trees, and he undid more of the buttons on his coat. They rounded a slight curve, and saw a metal gate chained and padlocked blocking the driveway. Jesse stopped. The fence extended in both directions as far as he could see. Both the gate and fence were topped with razor wire.

    A small sign was posted on the right post of the gate. It read, 'Property of the US Government. STAY OUT Trespassers will be prosecuted to the full extent of the law.' The sign was ominous.

    Jesse bent over and examined two small yellow signs attached to the gates. The international symbol for biohazards was clearly marked. Jesse started backing up still facing the gates, staring at the signs. He almost bumped into Mark.

"What's wrong, Dad?"

"Those signs say we're in deep shit, Mark. Cole, lead us back to the truck. Walk and maintain your spacing like we did coming in to this place."

    They reversed their course and Cole led them to the truck. Cole climbed back up top,

Mark climbed in the back, and Jesse took the passenger seat in the cab.

"Get us out of here," Jesse said, and Sarah drove off.

"What was it?" Sarah asked.

"It was just some of your Government dollars at work. It turns out this road does lead somewhere. That place was a Biohazard Center. It looked deserted to me."

Sarah shook her head. "With all the problems we were having, those idiots were building biological weapons. That's probably why those local yokels wanted nothing to do with following us or this road."

Five miles and twenty minutes later, another driveway appeared on the right side of the road. Same as before, Jesse, followed by Mark and Cole, disappeared up the driveway.

Just as Jesse suspected, he stopped in front of a padlocked gate with the same razor wire on top. The fence again extended off in both directions. The same 'STAY OUT' sign was on the post. This time the yellow signs on the gates were the international symbol for radioactive material. Jesse directed their strategic withdrawal, and again climbed back in the truck.

"Well?" Sarah asked.

Friends of the Family

"It appears that this road's a real witch's brew. That one was posted as radioactive. We definitely know why the Government built this road. I can hardly wait to see what's next," Jesse said.

Just as Jesse predicted, twenty minutes later Sarah pulled to a stop even with a third driveway. Again Jesse, Mark, and Cole disappeared into the entrance. But this time, when Jesse rounded a slight curve, he was surprised when the road continued into the woods.

After another quarter mile and another slight curve in the road, Jesse came to stop in front of a gate that was different than the others. It was massive. Both the gate and the fences were twice as high and again topped with razor wire. The fence and gates appeared much more heavily constructed as well. Mark walked up by his dad and stopped. They both gazed up at the massive entrance.

"Gees, it looks like the wall in that movie," Mark said.

"What movie was that?"

"King Kong."

Jesse noted that the same government property sign was posted on the right pole holding the enormous fence. He stared hard at the signs on the gate.

'Beware of Dog'.

Jesse knew Sarah would probably be worried because they'd been gone much longer this time. They came walking in the center of the driveway and up to the truck. Jesse climbed into the cab and started chuckling to himself. Sarah looked at Jesse like he'd lost his mind. "What's so funny?"

"Do you remember when we first got married, and you had that ratty little dog?" Jesse asked.

"You mean Muffy? And it wasn't a ratty little dog, it was a toy poodle."

"Whatever. Do you remember the sign I bought you as a joke?" Jesse asked.

Sarah smiled. "Yes. The *'Beware of Dog'* sign. We put it up on the backyard fence. I think I remember you chasing me up the stairs after that..."

"Guess what sign was on that gate?" Jesse asked.

"You're kidding!"

"Not one like it, mind you. That exact same sign," Jesse said.

"What do you think it means?" Sarah asked.

"I have no idea, but I can't wait to find out what's next."

Friends of the Family

They drove another fifteen miles without encountering anymore driveways.

Finally they stopped by an isolated lake with trees came that grew all the way to the edge. It was a small lake, but appeared dark blue and deceptively deep. It had warmed considerably during the day, and everyone was tired and hungry. They decided to stay where they were for the night.

Both Sarah and Jesse no longer felt they were being watched. They were also encouraged by the absence of driveways, and felt the worst was behind them. They relaxed and sat studying the map, after everyone finished eating. Lily played with her plastic horse she'd named Tony. Sarah sent the three boys down to wash up in the lake. Cole took his rifle just in case.

"What do you think?" Jesse asked, looking up from the map.

"If I'm reading this right, I'd say this road continues for another thirty miles. Let's see. That would dump us out at Pine Knot, Kentucky. That can't be more than ten miles from the Tennessee border," Sarah said.

"This road may have been creepy, but it took two weeks off this trip. You did good, sweetheart, finding it."

All three boys came laughing and hollering as they returned from washing up. Sarah and Jesse thought they were beginning to see a real change in Cole. It had been some time since either of them had seen Cole smile, let alone laugh.

It was getting toward dusk, and Jesse started a fire. The boys began nodding off, and Sarah sent them to bed. They were asleep before their heads hit the pillows. Lily was dressed in her nightgown. Jesse and Sarah sat with her for a while in front of the fire.

"Mommy, how far are we from Heaven?" Lily asked as she clutched Tony to her chest.

"Lily, we're going to Haven, not Heaven," Sarah said with a smile.

"Oh" Lily said. "I thought Grandma and Grandpa would be there."

"No. We'll all have to wait a while before we get to see them. Okay?" Sarah said. Lily nodded her head.

"Lily, do you want to go to bed or stay up? Daddy and I are going to go down by the lake."

"Me and Tony will just sit here and watch the fire," Lily said.

Sarah went and got some towels and the bar of soap. She and Jesse walked slowly toward the lake arm in arm.

"It's a little brisk for a dip isn't it?" Jesse asked.

"Not if we move quickly," Sarah said. "Besides, you're starting to become the other side of ripe, if you know what I mean."

It was a cool, but beautiful night with a soft breeze. The trees rustled as a new moon rose and the surface of the lake shivered with the silver reflection.

Jesse was the first out and shook with the cold as he put on his clothes. Sarah joined him on the shore and they kissed. She toweled off, and they were both ready to return to the warm fire. They strolled slowly enjoying the quiet of the night and the closeness of each other.

As they approached the edge of the trees, they could see the fire and Lily with her hand outstretched as if reaching for something. Then they could hear Lily speaking to someone. They walked a little farther, and they could clearly hear what Lily was saying.

"Here doggy, doggy...Nice doggy."

chapter 10

Sarah shoved Jesse back into the trees and whispered, "Stay here…" She emerged from the trees and walked slowly towards the fire.

"Lily, Honey? What are you doing?" Sarah asked, trying to keep her voice calm as her heart raced with fear.

"Just talking with my new friend."

Sarah drew closer to the light of the fire. A wave of terror washed over her. Lily was standing by the front of the truck. Three feet in front of Lily was an enormous dog. Black as coal, with a broad massive head, and deep chest, it was heavily muscled on the neck, shoulders and flank. The dog sat staring at Lily at eye level.

As Sarah approached, the dog began following her with golden eyes reflecting the light from the fire. She walked around the fire and sat with her back to Lily and the dog.

The dog stood.

"Lily, why don't you come over here and sit down by me?" Sarah asked a slight nervous quiver in her voice.

Her hand was shaking noticeably as she slowly reached to pick up a stick from the fire. It was smoking on one end as Sarah poked the coals. She looked back over her shoulder and smiled at Lily and the dog.

"Please, Lily, come on over here and tell me all about your new friend," Sarah said softly.

"Okay," Lily said. She walked over and sat down next to her mother.

Sarah continued to hold onto the stick, wondering what to do next. She at least had Lily away from the dog. Her hand trembled, the stick painting blue-smoky lines in the air. Sarah glanced back towards the massive dog. The dog stared back, and then plodded slowly over by the fire, close to Sarah.

It sat, looking directly at Sarah. Very gently, the dog took the stick from Sarah's hand with its mouth, and dropped it back in the fire. The dog then sunk to the ground next to Sarah, put its massive head on its paws, and closed its eyes.

Friends of the Family

Sarah noticed she hadn't been breathing. "That certainly is a nice doggy, Lily. Jesse? Would you like to join us now? Oh, and as a suggestion? I'd move real slow if I were you."

Jesse walked out of the trees, towards the fire.

"No problem," Jesse said. "But do you mind if I bring a couple of friends with me?"

Jesse approached the fire followed by two more dogs. Both dogs were almost as large as the first. It seemed to Sarah that this was planned, somehow. The dogs were escorting Jesse. Jesse knelt by the fire across from Sarah and Lily. The two dogs lowered to the ground on either side of Jesse. After a few minutes they put their heads on their front paws and closed their eyes.

"Well, isn't this special," Sarah said.

"It just keeps getting better and better," Jesse replied. "More dogs heading this way."

Off to the right, two more large black dogs walked out of the darkness and up to the fire. The smaller one went over to Lily and laid its head on Lily's lap. Lily stroked the dog's head gently. The dogs by Jesse rose to their feet, stretched, and trotted out of camp. As if on signal, one turned left and the other right. They disappeared into the woods on either side of the road.

"I'm not certain, but I think this one's pregnant." Sarah said, pointing towards the dog with its head in Lily's lap.

"They act like they know what each other is thinking," Jesse said.

Sarah glanced up and saw Cole peek over the top of the truck. Cole slowly reached out and took hold of his rifle. The big dog next to Sarah picked up his head, and stood. He looked up at where Cole lay. Sarah cleared her throat.

"Ah, Cole, let's not do anything rash. In fact, why don't you wake Mark up and tell him the same thing. Just don't make any threatening moves, and for God's sake, don't pick up a weapon. There's something odd about these dogs, and there are more of them are out in the dark."

Cole did as he was told, and Mark came climbing out of the cab, still half asleep. When he saw the dogs, his jaw dropped open.

"What the..." Mark said.

"Mark," Sarah said as calmly as she could, "We've got some company. They seem calm enough. Just walk slowly, and don't make any threatening moves."

"Threaten them? I could ride this big one without a saddle! That's the biggest dog I've ever seen," Mark exclaimed.

Friends of the Family

"Well, so far they just seem to want to be close to the fire," Jesse said.

"I'm not so sure," Sarah replied. "I think they want to be close to us."

The pregnant female with her head on Lily's lap began snoring. Lily giggled. "She sounds just like Daddy. I think I'll name her Daisy."

Mark walked over to the door of the truck and stuck his head in. "Paul, wake up. We got some friends out here you should meet," Mark said relishing the surprise.

Paul came to the door and climbed out, rubbing his eyes with sleep. He yawned until he saw the dogs. "Holy Cow! Where'd the dogs come from?" Paul asked.

The big dog by Sarah continued to stare up at Cole. It seemed to her, the dog never blinked. She reached out tentatively and patted his head. Still the massive dog didn't move.

"Cole, why don't you come down here?" Jesse asked.

"You're sure?" Cole asked.

"No, I'm not sure. But you're making this big one nervous. They must have walked in here for a reason. Let's just hope they've decided not to eat us," Jesse said. "Besides the boss here isn't going to relax until you do."

Cole climbed down, and stood over by the truck, his hands clearly empty. The big dog Jesse called Boss went back by Sarah and lay down by the fire and closed its eyes.

For an uncomfortably long time, the odd group sat like this around the fire. The only sound was Daisy's occasional snore. "If any of you have any ideas, the floor's open for suggestions," Sarah finally said.

Paul, Mark, and Lily all looked at their dad. Jesse looked puzzled.

"Let me recap," Sarah said. "We have four, no five, very large dogs in or around our camp. In fact, this very pregnant female appears especially fond of Lily. Her name's Daisy. Is that right Lily?"

Lily nodded her head and Daisy stopped snoring, opening one eye. After a moment the dog closed her eye and started snoring again.

"Now the one Jesse called Boss, takes special interest in any movement that appears threatening. Let's assume he is the boss. We have a young one over by Jesse, and two more out there somewhere doing God knows what. Anything you want to add?"

"They don't act like a pack of wild dogs," Mark ventured.

Friends of the Family

"They look well fed to me," Cole remarked.

"I've been thinking," Jesse commented. "These dogs have to be from that last stockade we saw. It could have been some sort of a genetics lab. It might mean they were a part of some government research project."

"Well, they don't appear to be in any hurry to leave. If they're part of some research project, I think we should backtrack to that last compound. See if we can find anything to tell us what's going on," Sarah said.

"We could just pile in the truck and leave them here....," Cole suggested hopefully.

"I don't think so Cole," Sarah answered. "This morning Lily and I saw something black moving in the woods, and came running back to the truck. I think what we saw was one of these dogs and they've been following us all day. If we just drive off, they may show up in our next camp as well. No, they walked in here for a reason. I think the answer is back in the compound. We have to go back."

"Well, not tonight," Jesse said. "We'll go back in the morning. Let's try to get some sleep."

Lily patted Daisy's head one more time and climbed into the truck, followed by Paul and Mark. Cole climbed back on the roof and under his tarp and Jesse and Sarah climbed into the truck cab. Sarah spent most of the night looking out the passenger window at the dogs. She watched the fire as it dwindled to glowing embers. Some time later, she fell asleep.

chapter 11

Sarah awoke with a start. The temperature had dropped during the night and the cab windows were fogged over. She rubbed the passenger window with the back of her hand, but it did little good. Heavy dew covered the outside of the window as well. She opened the door to the cab.

The dogs were gone. She felt oddly disappointed. They were scary, but not threatening. They made her feel secure for some strange reason, in spite of their appearance. And yet the dogs were a little too aware, a little too smart. Their actions seemed coordinated. She hoped there was an explanation back at the lab.

Jesse and the kids woke up a short time later. Except for Cole, Sarah thought they too were genuinely disappointed that the dogs had vanished. Lily seemed to be affected most of all. Sarah explained to her that the dogs liked living in the woods, and probably didn't like to ride in trucks. Lily wasn't buying any of it.

"Now what?" Jesse asked.

Sarah thought for a few moments. They could just leave and assume the dogs wouldn't follow them. But she felt certain they would see them again.

"We go back to the compound. I can't explain it Jesse, but I need to find out about those dogs. Call me crazy, but I miss them."

"Me too," Lily added.

"Okay, crazy. Let's eat," Jesse replied.

After breakfast, Jesse asked the boys to clean all their weapons, and reload the ammo clips. He put Cole in charge of the operation, while he and Sarah went for a short walk. They went a short distance and Sarah said she wanted to sit for a while and enjoy the morning. It was warming up rapidly.

"Jesse, I'm not positive at this point, but I don't think Daisy is the only one who's pregnant. I think we're going to have a baby," Sarah said.

"That's wonderful, Sarah! When will you know for sure?"

"Women react differently to stress, and this whole trip may have just thrown me out of kilter. I won't be sure for another week or so. But I'm worried."

"Oh, sweetheart, it will be fine. Once we get to Haven. We'll find a doctor or midwife to help you and everything will be alright."

"It's not that, Jesse. Women have been having babies naturally for thousands of years. It's just that I'm not exactly in my prime. Women my age aren't supposed to have babies. I'm a little old to be going through this and everything's so uncertain right now."

"Sarah, I love you, and we'll see this through just like everything else."

Jesse put his arms around her and held her gently for a while and Sarah started to feel better. The sun rose higher and the two walked back toward the truck holding hands. Everything was packed and Jesse and Sarah climbed in the cab. Jesse looked around, started the engine, and headed back towards the compound.

The truck stopped in front of the high gate and fences. Jesse honked the truck's horn several times, but nothing moved. Sarah noticed the surveillance cameras on the top of each gate post weren't pointed in their direction, and seemed fixed in place. They got out of the truck and walked to the fence.

"What do you think?" Jesse asked.

"This fence makes it looks like Jurassic Park. It looks abandoned. Can you push the gate in with the truck?"

"I think so," Jesse replied. "This place is really creepy. Are you sure you want to do this?"

"Just do it, Jesse."

Jesse told everyone to get out of the truck and nudged the front bumper against the center of the gate. The truck engine roared as the gate bowed. With the sound of breaking metal, the gates sprung open and the truck lurched into the compound. Jesse climbed out with his shotgun. Sarah joined him, followed by Lily and the boys. All headed towards a windowless single-story brick building, that sat at the end of a long circular drive.

As Sarah walked up the front walk she saw leaves and twigs piled in the front portico. The front door stood slightly ajar. Jesse went into the building first, followed by Mark and Cole, guns ready.

"Hello? Is anybody home?" Jesse yelled, his voice echoing in the empty building.

Sarah heard the echoes die as she and Lily walked into what appeared to be a reception area. Dust and dirt covered chrome end tables, mildewed leather chairs, and the counter top. Jesse and the boys disappeared through a heavy door standing slightly ajar at the far end of the room.

"Hey, wait for us," Sarah yelled as she and Lily stepped through the door.

Large skylights filtered light through the roof of the building and lit up the floating dust motes hovering in the air. Jesse and the boys stood just inside the door of what appeared to be a massive laboratory. At the far end was a row of large cages. The cage doors were open and the cages empty. A line of offices ran down the left hand side of the laboratory, each door labeled with a name plate. The first office was labeled in plain block letters 'Dr. Daniel Frank, Director'.

"What now?" Jesse asked.

"Let's see if Doctor Frankenstein's in," Sarah replied.

Jesse went over and tried the door. It was locked. Several kicks later, the door sill cracked and the door slammed open. Jesse stuck his head in and looked around.

"Nobody's home," Jesse said.

A small skylight lit the windowless room in somber shadows. Sarah stepped into the office and began going through the metal desk.

In the lower right hand drawer she found four unlabeled binders. She pulled the first one out of the drawer and read for a while in silence.

"Jesse, you were right. Those dogs came from here. Take the kids back to the truck. This could take me a while".

Jesse, the boys, and Lily headed back to the truck. Sarah joined them after an hour or so. She carried the four binders under her arm and handed them to Mark. "Put the binders in the back of the truck will you? You'll all need to hear this."

The family sat in a circle on the ground. Jesse finished fixing some lunch and they ate while Sarah related what she had learned about the dogs.

"Let's begin with the fact you were right, Jesse. Those dogs came from here. And yes, it's a government research facility specializing in genetic engineering. Four years ago, according Dr. Frank's meticulous notes, the military started a program to create the perfect guard dog. The dogs were to be used to combat terrorism. They thought they could come up with a dog to stop terrorists before they acted."

"Before they acted?" Jesse asked.

"The scientists proved that anyone under a great deal of stress could be detected by a subtle difference in smell, heart rate, and other

Friends of the Family

biological feedback by a trained, genetically altered dog. So they altered the genetics of the dogs for size, intelligence, disposition, and enhanced sensory perception. They didn't want to have to spend a lot of time training the dogs, so they genetically programmed the dogs too. The results walked into our camp last night."

"Did they succeed?" Mark asked.

"Yes. Apparently they succeeded too well," Sarah replied. "It appears from his notes that even before the go-back, things started to get strange. Certain lab workers and researchers were singled out by the dogs. According to Dr. Frank, each of the workers was subsequently proven to be masking some deviant qualities. One beat his wife and kids, another liked little boys too much, that sort of thing. The dogs didn't attack the workers. They simply didn't let them into the building. The dogs could not only spot bad intentions, they could identify bad people."

"How could they?" Jesse asked. "What basis would the dogs use to make that sort of judgment?"

"It isn't judgment, Jesse, its instinct. Dr. Frank used a lot of paper and ink towards the end putting down his thoughts. He felt there was a natural order to things. A balance if you will. The dogs are sensitive to that natural balance."

"I'm not sure I follow," Jesse said.

"He had some ideas on how the dogs could do it. Dr. Franks speculated that people, like all living things, give off a detectable aura of light. Medical Doctors already used this aura for diagnosis. He believed the dogs could detect the presence of this light."

"You're kidding," Jesse interjected.

"It's not that far-fetched, Jesse. We talk about how some people make bad first impressions, that sort of thing. We've all heard about people that animals just flat don't like. It's like that with the dogs. Except when the dogs don't like you, it's for a reason."

"What happens if the dogs don't like you?" Jesse asked.

"The good doctor suggested that if the dogs don't like you, you should probably make sure you're somewhere else."

"What else did he say?" Jesse asked.

"At the end, it was all very disjointed. His handwriting was shaky and you could tell he was under tremendous pressure. The researchers killed all but the five adult dogs. Somehow they got loose and no one could get close enough to them to put them down. Then after the go-back, the government evacuated all

Friends of the Family

of the compounds. Dr. Frank confessed at the end of the last book that he was the one that had released the five remaining dogs."

"Is there anything else we should know?" Mark asked.

"Well, just some minor things."

"Like what?" Jesse asked.

"They only eat food they catch in the wild. Apparently they could detect the chemicals farmers put into livestock. The researchers couldn't get them to eat it."

"Did this doctor happen to mention which food group people belonged to?" Cole asked smiling.

"Domesticated, Cole, the doctor was very specific about that," Sarah replied. "They might kill you…, but they won't eat you."

"Good news everybody, we're not on the menu! Is there anything else?" Jesse asked.

"Yes. They tend to travel in pairs and don't like being all at the same place at the same time. Dr. Frank felt this was some survival of the species instinct. He also said they're very territorial, and tend to patrol the perimeter of what they consider to be their territory just like wolves do."

"Wolves, gees, this just gets better and better," Cole muttered under his breath.

"They mostly breed true," Sarah continued, "but occasionally some of their pups may be genetic throwbacks. If they are, the dogs let them die. Oh, and they kill all other dogs entering what they consider their territory. The Doctor was very emphatic about this. No exceptions. They just don't tolerate other dogs. The researchers thought it was also some sort of species protection thing."

"Cole is right. These dogs are full of surprises. The question is what do you think we should do?" Jesse asked.

Sarah sat and thought for a while. She looked up finally and saw everyone looking expectantly, waiting for her answer.

"I can't explain it, but Dr. Frank trusted those dogs and so do I. He said they appeared to have a strong need for human companionship. I think that's why they came into our camp last night. We need all the help we can get. Jesse, I think those dogs chose us for a reason. I just feel it."

"Well if you're right, and I still have my doubts, the dogs are probably watching us right now," Jesse said. Everyone looked around and studied the trees outside the compound. Jesse stood up.

"It's too late to make any real distance today, so let's go back to where we camped

Friends of the Family

last night and see if they come back," Jesse said.

They drove slowly to the spot where they'd camped the previous night. Jesse built a campfire, and when the dogs failed to appear, everyone went to bed.

Sarah was the first up the next day. There was still no sign of the dogs. Jesse announced they would make Tennessee today and that they were getting very close to Haven. Sarah thought everyone's spirits picked up a little, although she still felt a sense of loss, when the dogs failed to return.

chapter 12

As the truck lumbered away from the camp site, Sarah found herself examining the woods for any sign of the dogs. A steep grade ran uphill for almost two miles. When the truck reached the top of the ridge, the road made a sharp left, then right. As they came around the last turn, Jesse slowed the truck.

"Will you look at that?" Jesse said. All five dogs sat on the right-hand shoulder of the road, side by side, in a straight row. "If they pick up their paws and try thumbing a ride, I'm going to flip out. What do you suggest we do?"

Sarah thought for a moment. "Tell you what. Pull up, and I want to get out."

"Are you sure, Sarah?" Jesse asked.

"Yes. All my intuitions are screaming these dogs are important to us and our safety. I'm not going anywhere without them. I know you may think this is a needless risk, but I just know these dogs are important to us. Now stop the damn truck!"

"Gee's, you don't have to...," Jesse said, shaking his head.

Sarah mumbled *'Oh, kiss my...'*, as she got out of the truck and slammed the door. The dogs trotted single-file over to where she stood. Boss stood on the far right. Next to him was Daisy. The rest appeared to be ordered by size. Sarah estimated that Boss stood about 3 feet to the top of his head. He weighed easily 180 pounds. His head looked to be a foot wide, his jaws were massive.

There was an oddly intelligent gleam in all their eyes, as they repositioned themselves in a semicircle around Sarah at a respectful distance. She stood with her back to the cab door. Sarah got the distinct impression they were in some sort of formation. It was as if they wanted to reassure her, they were not a threat. They all stared up at her.

"Who called this meeting, and what do you want?" Sarah asked the dogs, joking, and half expecting them to laugh. Instead, Boss walked over to the side of the truck, jumped up and put his front paws on the door. He stared back at Sarah.

Friends of the Family

"That seems clear enough. Kids, open the door and come out. We're going to have to do some rearranging," Sarah said.

Boss jumped down and rejoined the semi-circle, and the truck door opened. Cole finally peered over the edge of the roof at the commotion below.

"Wow! They're back," Paul said as he jumped out. Mark and Lily followed.

"Mark? You and Paul climb up on top with Cole. Lily, you ride up front with your Dad and me."

"Can't I ride in back with Daisy?" Lily asked.

"I don't think so, Lily. Maybe you can later."

Lily climbed into the cab, as the boys scurried up the rope ladder to join Cole on the roof of the truck. Sarah watched the dogs file over to the door. Boss waited as Daisy and the rest jumped into the truck before he followed. She closed the door and climbed back into the cab. When Jesse looked at her Sarah just shrugged.

"Did Dr. Frank happen to mention who taught them close order drill?"

"Just drive," Sarah said, looking out the side window.

The road ran smooth with no more driveways or surprises. Sarah was kept busy stopping Lily from sticking her head through the opening from the cab into the back to see what the dogs were doing.

Boss ended the contest by wedging his huge head into the cab. Jesse almost lost control when he looked over and Boss gave him a blast of dog breath in the face. Lily was delighted and patted Boss's head.

"You realize anyone looking into the cab will think we have a bear's head mounted on the back of the cab," Jesse said.

Sarah laughed. "Believe it or not, I think Boss just wants to see where we're going. If you think I'm going to try and shove his head back through that hole, forget it," Sarah said.

By midday, the concrete road came to a dead-end at what used to be a major highway. Jesse headed southeast, straight for the Tennessee border.

The new road rapidly narrowed with disabled and abandoned vehicles on both shoulders. Jesse slowed to a crawl to make his way through the burned out cars and trucks littering the road. At several spots twisted wreckage blocked the road entirely. Jesse plowed through the vehicles to clear a path. They came to a 'Welcome to Tennessee' sign extending high above the road. The sign was riddled with bullet holes and covered with graffiti. One of the messages scrawled *'Now go back home, Tennessee don't want you either'*.

A mile into Tennessee another sign read 'Welcome Center' and someone hand painted 'is closed' underneath. The Welcome Center was burnt to the ground. Cars continued to litter the road. Jesse pressed on, and asked Sarah to study the map again for a place to stop.

"The map shows an entrance to a wilderness camping area up ahead about five miles. I don't see any marked roads though. It might be a good place to get off and stop. Do you want to try?" Sarah asked.

"That sounds like what we're looking for."

Sarah noticed that many of the cars sitting at all angles on the shoulder of the road were riddled with bullet holes. She'd also peered into some of the cars as they crept slowly by. Inside were disturbingly lumpy piles of clothing. Sarah figured the cars must have been here for a while, but she was getting less enthused about this road with every mile.

The cut off to the wilderness area was unmarked. Jesse drove by it the first time and was forced to back up to find it. Cars and a single pickup truck blocked much of the entrance.

Sarah suggested that Jesse squeeze between them, without moving anything. She saw no point in advertising they'd gone this way.

Once they'd gone about two miles inside the park, the abandoned cars thinned out and disappeared. Jesse drove until they found a fire break. When they were out of sight, he shut the engine off, climbed out, and opened the door to the truck. The dogs came out in the same order as they went in. Boss emerged last. Immediately all the dogs but Daisy disappeared into the brush. Each dog headed in a different direction. Daisy rested by the edge of the firebreak.

That evening, two of the dogs returned, and joined the family and Daisy around the fire. As the darkness set in, Boss and the last dog trotted into camp, each carrying something in their mouths. As the younger dogs rose and left the camp, Boss walked up to Daisy and deposited a mauled rabbit in front of her. The second dog dropped a dead rabbit in front of Sarah as well. Daisy picked her rabbit up and bit down hard several times. With the sound of bones breaking, she pulverized it and devoured the thing in a single gulp.

Sarah picked up the rabbit in front of her, by a back leg using two fingers and dropped it in front of Daisy. "Here's your dessert. I'll be over in the bushes for a few minutes."

Sarah ran for the woods with her hand over her mouth. The sounds emerging from the trees, told everyone she was losing her lunch. She returned a short time later with as much dignity as she could and sat down by Jesse.

"Well that was a Kodak moment," Sarah said.

"Yes indeed. Are you all right?"

"I am now. I wonder why they thought I needed a special gift."

"I'm not sure about anything with the dogs. They may sense something about you, Sarah. Felt you and Daisy needed a little extra food for some reason."

Sarah smiled at Jesse. "Well, they apparently have joined the family."

"I wonder. Do they think they joined us or that we joined them?"

"Either way, I'm glad they're here," Sarah said. "Mark, would you reach in the back of the truck and see if you can find me something to eat? Suddenly I'm starving."

chapter 13

Jesse wasn't surprised the next morning, when the dogs lined up at the truck door. He and Sarah had discussed the dogs last night. If Sarah had to choose between him and the dogs, Jesse was pretty sure he would lose.

They'd also decided to return to the highway and take it as far south as possible. The map showed the road passing very close to a cutoff to Haven. He knew at the first sign of trouble, they might have to reconsider using the highway. Jesse backtracked to the highway and eventually began to make good time. He slowed as they approached the town of Linden.

He remembered visiting Linden as a small boy with his father and mother. It was the first time he'd slept overnight in someplace besides his own bedroom. All he could remember was a picture over the bed of a deer standing by a lake surrounded by woods and mountains. He'd loved that picture. It had been painted on a piece of wood with the bark still on it. He vaguely remembered his mother visiting a doctor on that trip. But it was all fuzzy, and he wasn't sure.

As Linden came into view, Jesse felt he was looking at a western movie set. He stopped at the first building on the edge of town.

"Sarah, would you look at this?" Jesse asked.

They both sat staring at the main street of Linden. Horses were tied to old parking meters. Buggies and wagons moved up and down the street. A wagon approached, with an old man and little boy sitting on the seat. Two large horses clopped along as the wagon first approached, then went by Jesse and Sarah.

The old man stared at the truck and shook his head for no apparent reason. A shotgun lay across his lap. The little boy looked up at the roof of the truck and waved tentatively. Jesse and Sarah watched in the side rearview mirrors as the wagon continued up the highway away from town.

"I think it must have looked like this, a hundred years ago," Sarah said, astounded by what she saw.

Friends of the Family

"Actually, my Dad still farmed with mules when I was a little boy," Jesse replied. "But you're right. It's most peculiar."

Jesse shut the truck down and told the boys to stay where they were. He, Sarah, and Lily got out of the cab, and walked towards the market set up in the middle of the street. It was the center of activity.

Jesse and Sarah drew attention primarily because of his long canvas coat and they were new in town. They walked past little stands with handmade crafts for sale. Many candles, cakes, rugs, and quilts were displayed. Some fresh vegetables were displayed, but not many. Sarah commented it was still too early in the year.

They stood and watched two women, who resembled each other like sisters, examine some large white candles. The sisters appeared to be in a friendly discussion with the young girl behind the table. They came to an agreement, and the older sister reached deep into a large cloth sack she carried, and pulled out a chicken by the feet and set it on the table.

The chicken wore a small sack over its head, and didn't move from where it was placed. The girl nodded and picked the chicken off the table and set it on the ground under the table. The sisters considered the table full of candles for some time. They each selected a candle, not so tall as squat. The candles disappeared into the large cloth sack, and the sisters waved at the smiling girl as they walked on.

Jesse felt a tap on his shoulder.

"New in town?" a voice said. It was a man perhaps ten years older than Jesse. He was also considerably shorter and heavier, with a ruddy face and squinty eyes. His build was stocky and powerful. His hand rested lightly on a holstered gun.

"Yep," Jesse answered. "I've been here before, though. It was over thirty years ago. My parents brought me here with them. I don't recall there being this many horses."

"The horses are new. Might say it's a giant step backward for this part of the country," the man said.

Lily ran up to Sarah and looked at the man talking to her parents.

"Jesse, why don't you introduce us to this gentleman?" Sarah said. "Mister…?"

"My name's Jasper…Jasper Thiggs," the man said removing his hat.

"Well, Jasper Thiggs, meet my wife Sarah and daughter Lily."

"I'm pleased to meet you. You say your name's Jesse?"

"Yes, Jesse Colter. I'm originally from down by Eagle Rock."

"I'm the law around here. Eagle Rock, you say? Been there recently?"

"No. It's been a couple of years since I've been to the old place," Jesse said.

"Just a second...Luther, stop sneaking around and come over here so I can introduce you. Excuse me, but my boy thinks he's being clever. He's my deputy, and he still has a lot to learn," Jasper said.

"Why Jasper, you don't know how pleased we are to finally see some law and order," Sarah said with a smile.

"Thanks, Mrs. Colter, not everybody feels that way. How bout you Jesse, you glad to see the law?"

"Usually," Jesse said. "Mr. Thiggs, maybe those other two men trying to get up behind us could come over and we could all get acquainted."

The stocky Jasper smiled. "Call me Jasper. You got a good eye, Mr. Colter. Maybe you could have the boy on the roof of your truck take the scope off me."

"Call me Jesse. Cole, relax!" Jesse yelled back towards the truck.

"Alright Jesse, meet my son Luther. Luther, meet Jesse Colter, his wife Sarah, and their daughter Lily." Luther was a younger version of his father. He also was short, with reddish coloring and powerful build. Jesse shook his hand.

"I believe Lily and I will look around gentlemen," Sarah said. "Do us all a favor, and figure out which one's bigger peaceably."

The gathering group of men watched as Sarah and Lily walked up to the nearest stall.

"Well, Jesse, looks like we got to learn to get along," Jasper said with a smile.

"Seems so."

"Mind if we take a look in your truck?" Jasper asked.

"No, I don't mind, but I'd advise against it."

"How so?" Jasper asked.

"I got five of the biggest dogs you've ever seen in that truck. We're comfortable with them, but I'm just not sure how they would react to you."

Jesse looked back at the truck. "Hey, Boss!"

Boss stuck his head into the cab. Jasper took a step back.

"Good God! You sure he's not a bear?"

Friends of the Family

"Why, he's the runt of the litter," Jesse said. "He's the only one whose head can fit through the hole."

A small crowd began to gather as they talked. A murmur ran through the crowd when Boss stuck his head out. This brought an even bigger crowd.

"Jesse, are you planning on staying for a while?" Jasper asked.

"No. We're moving on. Just wanted to see what civilization looked like. We need to get to our place by Eagle Rock."

Jasper pursed his lips deep in thought.

"I'd go easy down there if I were you. A bad crowd lives in Eagle Rock. Vicious mean folk. Make sure you watch out for wild dogs around here too. We've got a real problem with packs raiding farms. You seem like decent folks, so I thought I ought to warn you."

"I appreciate that," Jesse said. "But it's our home and the sooner we get to Haven the happier we all will be. I have an old couple, Franklin and Hattie Pierce, living on the place. Have you heard anything about them?"

"Can't say that I have," Jasper said. "If you're set on leaving, you can turn down that street you just passed and out of town. Don't want you to scare the horses with that truck of yours."

Joel Baker

The men shook hands, and Jesse headed back to the where the boys now stood. Sarah and Lily returned a short time later, and Jesse did as Jasper suggested and bypassed the town.

They drove the rest of the afternoon. Jesse thought that judging by the quantity of road apples they passed horses were the only traffic they could expect to encounter. He began looking for the cutoff to Eagle Rock just south of Linden. He drove slowly and barely recognized the road when it appeared suddenly. It was twenty miles to Eagle Rock from the cutoff and Haven was three miles north of Eagle Rock.

The road was in bad shape and Jesse didn't want to try the dirt road at night, so he told Sarah to keep an eye out for someplace to stop. It was almost dark when Sarah saw a lane that disappeared into some heavy woods. The road was high with weeds and appeared deserted. Jesse pulled a hundred yards into the woods, and found an almost level place to park the truck.

Sarah turned the dogs loose, and they repeated the routine from the night before. This included the rabbits and finished with the same results. Jesse felt everyone's excitement

Friends of the Family

about being this close to the end of the journey.

All the dogs except for Daisy were gone from the camp when everyone turned in for the night. Daisy begged to get into the truck when Lily went to bed and Sarah decided to try it. Lily went to sleep using Daisy as a pillow. Daisy snored most of the night.

Just before dawn, Jesse came wide awake. Something caused Sarah to wake as well. They sat listening to the sounds of deep woods. Suddenly the night sounds stopped and everything went too quiet. Not a sound. Some distance away Jesse heard the crashing of brush, and the yelp of a dog, then a second crash and the high whine of a dog in pain. The second encounter sounded closer. A few minutes later he heard a third yelp and a loud crack. The same sound that Daisy made when she crushed a rabbit. Then silence returned. Jesse waited and a few minutes later the crickets and frogs resumed their spring soundings.

The next morning all four of the dogs sat staring at the truck door. Sarah woke Daisy and the dogs held a small reunion outside the truck. The boys peered over the top at the dogs below.

"Did anybody else hear that ruckus last night?" Mark asked.

"I think we all did," Jesse said, kneeling down by the dogs to examine them. "It sounded like they took care of some business. I don't see a scratch on the friends here."

Jesse stood and looked around. "I got good news everybody. Tonight we sleep at Haven! Now all aboard, cause this train is leaving!"

chapter 14

THREE MILES SOUTH of Haven, Calvin Haskin sat at a table inside the Shadow Bar and Grill. It was one of the few businesses still open in Eagle Rock. With Calvin sat his twin brother, Clarence, and his little brother, Teddy. Sam Greeley, the owner of the Shadow, opened the doors each morning, and swept the front walk occasionally. Since Calvin and his brothers had settled in, business had suffered.

Calvin and Clarence were always together. If the truth be known, Clarence really wasn't Calvin's twin. People thought they were, but they'd been born three months apart. They looked like each other, had the same papa, but their mothers had been sisters. Papa Haskin liked to tell his sons he believed in keeping it in the family. He took as a special pride in telling anyone who would listen; he'd been once described by a minister as *'someone who was mad, bad, and dangerous to know'*.

Calvin and Clarence were physically large people, who fed off each other's cruelty. Three months earlier, they'd beaten a man to death with axe handles in the street, in front of the bar. They were both so out of breath when they were through they'd vowed to get in better shape.

Their muscle had turned to fat some years before. Except for the runt Teddy, all the members of the Haskin clan had been of generous proportion. But it was their smell that people first noticed. Before the go-back, everyone used to speculate on the cause of the fetid odors. Some thought it must be diet, but most believed it was a lack of hygiene. Still others blamed the disgusting pomade they used to slick back their hair.

Calvin knew he and Clarence were a tad unusual in their conduct and demeanor. Dirt poor and with the twisted cunning of a rat, Calvin was most definitely the leader. But, while he would never admit it out loud, Calvin was really scared of his little brother Teddy. He'd given Teddy the nickname of *Weasel* and it had stuck. It just fit him so well, and he was simply, quite mad.

Friends of the Family

Teddy suffered the fate of most runts of the litter. Papa Haskin had seemed to take special pleasure in hitting him too hard and too often. It had turned Teddy insanely cruel. Calvin, like everyone, always watched his back when Teddy was around.

It seemed to Calvin that Teddy had always been a problem. It was rumored, when he was ten years old, he'd murdered a neighbor girl in a hideous fashion. It wasn't true. He was nine at the time.

Calvin studied his little brother through bleary eyes and a pounding headache. Teddy's hat was pulled down over his dirty hair in a way that made his ears stand out to the sides. Teddy thought his thick glasses, with the Buddy Holly frames, made him look smart. Everyone else thought they made him look deranged. The frames, broken several times, were fixed with gray duct tape.

"*Yep,*" Calvin thought. "*Having Teddy for a brother was like having a rabid dog for a pet. We're going to have to do something eventually.*" Right now, Calvin was hung over and had other concerns. Teddy looked bored. Nobody wanted to be around when Teddy got bored.

"Is this all we're going to do?" Teddy asked. His shrill voice was like a needle in the brain.

"Jesus, Teddy. We're so hung over we can barely sit upright, for Christ's sake," Calvin said.

"Yeah, give it a rest will ya?" Clarence chimed in. "We're dying here."

"You two were running around last night weren't you?" Teddy asked. "You guys never ask me to do anything."

"Ain't no big deal. We were out visiting some of the neighbors," Calvin replied. "If you'd been here you could a gone too."

"Yeah, Teddy, you missed a good time. Where were you?" Clarence asked.

"I was training my dogs," Teddy said.

The odd look on Teddy's face made Calvin wince. He and Clarence exchanged looks. They both knew how Teddy trained his fighting dogs, and the dried blood on Teddy's tee shirt told a story all its own.

"I told you if you don't stop torturing those dogs, they going to tear you up," Calvin said, hoping someday they would. "Now go find that prick bar owner, and tell him me and Clarence need whiskey or we're going to bust his head. Then go get Cassy to clean this shit house. Tell her she better keep her pie hole shut too. My head's killing me," Calvin said.

Teddy stood and slouched towards the back rooms where they kept Cassy locked up. Clarence watched his little brother until he was well out of sight, and then turned back to Calvin as he spoke. "Do you think it's a good idea to let Teddy around the girl?"

Calvin thought for a few moments. "He may mess with her some, but I don't think he would kill her. Besides, he likes little girls, not big ones like that bitch out back."

"He ain't getting any better. He keeps it up and one or both of us will wind up dead. Besides, all we do is steal people's food and bang their women. How many dead families we found? He keeps it up, and we're going to run out of people to feed us."

"I know, I know. I think he suspects us of planning something. You know how he is. But I think I can still control him."

"You damn well better," Clarence said, thinking for a minute. "You know what we need Calvin? We need more new people to move here. And we need Teddy to stop killing the ones that are already here."

"Well, people are starting to move around more. Worse case, we may have to move on. Either way, keep an eye on Weasel. I'll do the same."

***

Cassy sat on the edge of her filthy bed, inside the barren little room in the back of the Shadow Bar and Grill. She thought about her really bad decision to come live with the Haskin brothers as she studied herself in the cracked mirror hung on the wall. She looked ancient for seventeen and in a sorry state.

Her clothes were filthy and torn, the right breast exposed to the nipple. Her left eye was purple and swollen shut. Her stringy brown hair was bedraggled. She was tired of being passed back and forth between the brothers. Little Teddy gave her the creeps, and she didn't know how much more of this she could take. She just wanted it over, one way or another.

The decision to move in with the Haskin brothers had probably not been all that well thought out. Up until then she'd lived her whole life in a small ramshackle cabin about four miles south of town, down a long dirt path. Since her mother had died the year before of some sickness, she'd lived with just her little brother and pa. It had been a hardscrabble life before her mother died. It was worse after.

Pa had been after her in an unnatural way even before her mother was in the ground. She'd do about anything to be rid of her daddy and that rat trap farm. At first Calvin and Clar-

Friends of the Family

ence had been real nice to her. They'd given her presents and everything. The rutting had been difficult but she'd had boys up on her before, not to mention her pa. Momma had told her to just lay still and it was all over quick enough. Still these brothers were a dirty and disgusting bunch. Then they'd started knocking her around a lot.

Several days after she'd left home her pa happen to walk in when Calvin had her laid face down on a table, going at her. Pa didn't say anything, other than to complain he deserved something for the loss of his daughter's help on the farm. Calvin never even stopped doing her, when he told pa he'd make sure he got what he deserved. A short time later, the old cabin burned. Daddy and little brother were found inside the rubble. Thinking about her little brother made her sad.

Cassy stood up, suddenly alert. She heard someone shuffle up to her locked door, and the sound of a key turning. Teddy walked in and leered at her.

"Cassy, Calvin says for you to clean up the mess you all made last night, and he says to be quiet."

"Okay," Cassy said, waiting for Teddy to leave first, and then following. As she came through the door, he stood grinning at her.

When she walked by him with her head averted, Teddy pinched her hard on her bottom.

"Leave me alone. Please," she said through clenched teeth, as she pulled away from him. He'd meant it to hurt and now she'd have another purple bruise.

Teddy laughed in a high girlish giggle, making her skin crawl. She shuddered as she entered the room where Calvin and Clarence sat nursing their headaches. She shuffled over to far side of the room where a broom leaned against the wall and began sweeping the debris on the floor into a neat pile. Cassy tried making herself as small as possible.

chapter 15

JESSE WAS ANXIOUS to get the last leg of the trip out of the way. The dogs were in the back of the truck with Sarah and Lily. Mark and Cole were up top. He asked Paul to ride up front with him. They pulled out of the wooded lane, onto the small dirt road, and headed toward Haven. The closer they got, the more memories flooded back to Jesse.

His father and he were never especially close. Jesse remembered harsh words and the occasional belt strapping in the barn. Usually it was about work or something that needed to be done on the place. Jesse felt it was probably why he'd stayed away so long from the old homestead.

He'd loved his mother dearly. She'd done what she could to deflect some of his father's harshness away from Jesse. Though she was a soft and gentle person, she had a protective shell on the outside from hard work. His mother tried to make sure that some fun and joy was in Jesse's life. Jesse believed his father had loved his mother, which made her life a lot easier. Still when they'd died suddenly, they'd both left a hole in Jesse's heart.

"What are you thinking about Dad?" Paul asked.

"I was just thinking about my parents and when they died."

"What do you remember?"

"Not much really. More like impressions than memories. I was twelve, about your age. I was in bed, when I remember hearing a car pulling up outside our house. I remember thinking it was my Mom and Dad. They used to go into town to a little bar in Eagle Rock. They had live country music on Friday nights, and my parents would go to listen. I was by myself when I heard a pounding on the door."

"Who was it?" Paul asked.

"It was the police. I jumped up and answered the door. The first thing I noticed was the red and blue lights from the squad car flashing through the front door. The sheriff told me both my parents were killed in a car accident. Just like that. Apparently, they'd run off the road and hit a tree. When I saw the car lat-

Friends of the Family

er, it had blue paint smeared down the side. I'd asked the sheriff about it, but he'd said it was nothing. I always wondered about that blue paint."

"Why was that Dad?" Paul asked.

"My father was a fanatic about that car. He washed it all the time, and kept it spotless. I know there was no blue paint on the side of that car when they went to town."

"What happened then?" Paul asked.

"Well, I remember lots of people coming and going. Lots of casseroles dropped off. Friends of my parents, Franklin and Hattie moved out to the place to watch me until the authorities could find next of kin. My Dad was the last of his family, but my mother's sister lived up in Dayton. That was your great aunt Rose. Do you remember her?"

"Just a little bit," Paul said.

"Well, they contacted her and a couple of months after the funeral, put me on a bus for Dayton. All I took was a cheap suitcase and five dollars. Aunt Rose met me at the bus station. She was a really good person, but I was sure lonely," Jesse said.

"Gees, Dad, that must have been really tough," Paul said. "No matter how rough things are now, at least we're all together."

"It makes all the difference," Jesse said. They rode in silence for some time.

The closer they got to Haven, the more things were starting to look real familiar to Jesse. Mid-morning they stopped and stretched their legs. They let the dogs run a while and then everyone piled back in. Just about noon, Jesse slowed as he turned on to Sand Hill road headed towards Haskin Hill. The name Haskin jarred Jesse's memory.

He remembered a fight he'd had with the Haskin brothers shortly before his parents died. It was after school, just before the summer vacation when he was eleven or twelve. One of the twins said or did something to a girl Jesse liked, and made her cry.

Jesse called him out, knowing that you always got two for one with the Haskin brothers. Jesse held his own for a while. He'd bloodied the nose of one, and split the lip of the other one. He'd fought hard as he could. They were bigger and he was eventually pinned to the ground.

That was the first time his nose had been broken. For some reason, remembering that fight, all Jesse could focus on was the Haskin little brother. *What did they call him? Rat? No, it was Weasel,* Jesse thought. He could remember clearly the little kid with the thick glasses, giggling like a girl, as his older brothers kept hitting and kicking him.

"Welcome home, Jesse," Jesse muttered to himself.

"What was that?" Paul asked.

"We're here," Jesse answered.

As he slowed and finally spotted the lane back to Haven, Jesse flashed on one more distant memory about that fight. When the fight was almost over, a truck had pulled up. Old man Haskin got out and stood as his boys finished off Jesse. He didn't try to stop it, just stood watching. Jesse wasn't sure, but he seemed to recall that old man Haskin's truck was the same shade of blue as the streak on the side of his father's wrecked car.

Jesse turned into the entrance to Haven. It was about three hundred yards down a twisting hilly road, cut through the woods. It'd been some time since a truck this big had been down the road. The limbs scraped the truck. Jesse stopped just inside the entrance and told Cole and Mark to get down off the roof. He was afraid a tree limb might impale one of them. When they finally broke out of the woods, Jesse stopped. Sarah and Jesse climbed out of the truck and stood holding hands. The kids joined them and stood in silence.

A large secluded valley extended into the distance. It was just after noon, and the sunlight filtered down through the trees lining the edge of green grassy fields. The sound of rushing water came from their left. Jesse stood looking at the blue hazy hills receding into the distance. The sky was pale blue with white puffy clouds slowly drifting like ships on a sea.

"It's so beautiful!" Sarah exclaimed.

"Hey, everybody, come see this," Jesse said.

Sarah and the kids followed Jesse as he started down a small slope that skirted the start of the valley. They kept to a small footpath that meandered to a large cliff of red limestone. Beneath the cliff, water boiled out crystal blue and clear. The stream ran from under the cliff's face, down the valley, a full twenty feet wide and ten feet deep in the middle.

"Watch this," Jesse said.

Jesse knelt on one knee and drank deeply from the creek.

"It's the purest water you'll ever drink, ice cold too. I've really missed this water," Jesse said.

"Where does it come from?" Paul asked.

"No one knows for sure. A vast drainage area feeds a reservoir deep in the earth. The water chose this point to resurface. It carved this valley, and has never failed or slowed that I've ever heard of. This spot makes Haven special," Jesse said.

"Cole, go let the dogs out. Would you?" Sarah asked.

Cole headed up towards the truck, and a few moments later the dogs came down the path in single file. They drank one at a time, and lay down on the grassy bank.

"How big is this place, Dad? It looks huge," Paul asked.

Well, first you have to realize the valley's really shaped like an hour glass," Jesse said. "The ridges run almost due north and south. They curve in the middle like a waist. The cabin and out buildings are located at the waist where the ridges come together. The narrowest part of the valley's probably a mile wide. At the widest points, it's more like three miles. Overall, the valley runs north for about six miles. Let's go see if Franklin and Hattie are home. Let's get back in the truck, people."

The boys raced each other to the truck. The dogs followed single file in an orderly procession. Jesse drove down the right side of the valley along the eastern ridge.

As rooftops came into view, the smoke coming from the chimney of the smaller cabin was reassuring to Jesse. The rich smell of plowed earth wafted through the truck windows. Jesse could see that Franklin had a good start on the fields surrounding the cabins. Jesse pulled under a huge oak tree next to the main cabin and shut the engine off.

"Welcome to Haven, everybody," Jesse called out. "Cole. Mark. Ask the dogs to stay in the truck for now."

Jesse sounded the truck horn a few times, climbed out of the truck, and waited with Sarah. The screen door on the smaller cabin opened. Out stepped a large black man of about sixty years with hair that was mostly white. He was tall but didn't appear so, because he walked with a stoop. He wore bib overalls, a bright red shirt, and a straw hat that was more straw than hat. It was Franklin.

"Boy, you're a sight for sore eyes," Franklin said.

He walked up to Jesse, put his arms around him and lifted Jesse into the air. He then went to Sarah and took his hat into his hands.

"You must be Mrs. Colter. Please to meet ya," Franklin said.

"Call me Sarah. Franklin, we were worried about you and Hattie," Sarah said.

"Me and Hattie been worried about you all too. No way for us to get a hold a you, so nothing we could do but keep on, keeping on," Franklin said.

"Where's Hattie at, Franklin?" Jesse asked.

"Oh, she's in fixin herself, cause you're company. Hattie! Come on out here!" Franklin shouted back towards the house.

The door opened and a small black woman came out on the porch and walked towards the group under the oak tree. She appeared younger than Franklin, but not uncomfortably so.

"Hattie, you know Jesse, and this here's Sarah," Franklin said.

Sarah walked up to Hattie and gave her a hug.

"If first impressions mean anything, we're going to be fast friends," Sarah said.

Sarah introduced the children and Cole to Franklin and Hattie. Lily peeked from behind Sarah's legs, too shy to actually look at the new people.

"See Hattie, I told you they'd be here today," Franklin said.

"Yeah, and you was right. Course you been wrong everyday for two months, but today you was right," Hattie replied, making her point.

"Ouch!" Jesse said. "Franklin, it looks to me like we've met our match with these women."

"You got that right, Jesse," Franklin laughed. "Hattie's got some cornbread and ham inside if you're hungry. Jesse, maybe you and the boys want to eat before I show you around the place."

"Good idea, Franklin," Jesse said. "But first we need to finish the introductions. We brought some friends with us. They're still in the truck."

"What friends?" Franklin asked.

"Well, I need to ask you and Hattie something first," Jesse said.

"What?" Franklin asked, with a puzzled look on his face.

"How do you and Hattie feel about dogs? Big dogs?" Jesse asked.

Franklin and Hattie both looked at Jesse with concern.

"We got nothing against them, but we've had trouble with wild dogs round here. They come down at night and try messing with livestock and chickens. I keep chasing them out," Franklin said.

"How about you Hattie, are you afraid of dogs?" Jesse asked.

"Not especially. I do prefer little dogs to big dogs," Hattie said, a look of concern still on her face.

Friends of the Family

Jesse pointed to the front porch of the little cabin. "It might be a good idea for you both to go stand over there."

Once they were situated, he went to the truck and opened the side door. Boss was the first out, followed by Daisy and the rest of the dogs. Boss walked towards Franklin and Hattie. When he got about ten feet from the porch, Hattie disappeared into the house and looked through the screen door. Boss stopped and stared at Franklin. Franklin stared back.

"Franklin, you may as well blink first, because Boss can do that for hours. You should come on down and meet the friends. They're good dogs and they're not going to hurt you. Besides, I'm not big enough to make them leave," Jesse said.

Franklin came off the porch and took a tentative step towards Boss. Boss sat down and Franklin petted his head. The other dogs walked over toward Boss and Franklin.

"Hattie, come on out here. We got to get used to the dogs. They seem peaceable enough. Not like them wild ones," Franklin said.

Hattie's head poked out of the door. Sarah walked over to where the dogs and the men were.

"Come here Lily. Introduce Daisy to Hattie. With luck, Hattie, we'll have puppies around here real soon," Sarah said.

"Daisy, this is Hattie. Hattie, this is Daisy," Lily said with a smile.

"Oh Lord!" Hattie said as she emerged from behind the screen door. "I'll get used to them, I guess. But they're not coming into my house, and that's final."

Hattie reached out and patted Daisy lightly on the head.

"There are some things you need to know about the dogs," Jesse said. "The good news is that they don't eat livestock or people. They just eat wild food they hunt themselves."

"What you going to do if they do eat your chickens?" Hattie asked.

"Eat corn bread," Jesse answered. Everybody laughed.

They all headed for the small cabin. Daisy stayed close to Lily. Boss and the other three dogs each headed out in different directions as if a signal were given.

"Where are those dogs going?" Franklin asked.

"I have no idea," Jesse said. "Franklin, the dogs joined us on the trip down here. They're a little strange. We found some information on them but it was kind of sketchy. Both Sarah and I think they may be able to help us around here. Please tell me you don't have dogs, do you?"

"Naw. Hattie and me never really been that keen on dogs. Why?" Franklin asked.

"Well," Jesse said. "I'm not sure what we'd of done if you'd had a dog, Franklin, other than bury it. See, Franklin, they don't like other dogs either."

chapter 16

Lunch was delicious and went well. Hattie appeared much less nervous away from the dogs. After lunch, Hattie took Sarah and Lily out to the chicken coop, carrying a basket lined with a kitchen towel. Daisy followed them at a distance.

"Looks to me like this dog is going to have puppies within the week," Hattie said, glancing at Sarah for a moment. "Could be, we're going to have more than puppies around here before too long."

Sarah smiled to herself at Hattie's talent of observation. They entered the darkened coop. She was immediately struck with the smell of ammonia from the chicken dung. Straw covered the floor. Wood boxes hung from the walls with hinged lids, with holes cut in the front of each box. Trays of fine gravel sat on the floor.

"What's the gravel for?" Sarah asked.

"Chickens need gravel so they can chew," Hattie answered. "That's cause they don't have teeth."

Sarah left it at that, but made a mental note to ask Jesse if Hattie was pulling her leg. Poles for roosting were suspended by wire from the ceiling. Dim light filtered through windows covered with mesh wire.

Hattie showed Lily how to look for eggs. Sarah noticed that Lily was a little timid about the gentle art of lifting a sitting hen to see if she was on eggs. The shack, housing the chickens, had old rusty sheet metal around the building at the base. Hattie explained to Sarah it was added to try to keep wild animals from getting at the chickens.

Sarah watched as Lily warmed up to Hattie. Hattie's easy-going demeanor soon transformed the trip to the coop into an egg hunt. Lily laughed with delight with every egg she found. Hattie showed her how to dip cracked corn out of the barrel in the corner and pour it into the feeders along the walls.

"Next to horses, I like chickens best. I think I'm going to name this one Tulip," Lily said, as she started naming the chickens.

"Lily, honey, don't be naming the chickens," Hattie said shaking her head, "Cause

Friends of the Family

chickens are probably the dumbest animals God ever created."

As an aside to Sarah, Hattie whispered that they were having fried chicken for dinner that night and how she refused to eat anything that had a name.

Franklin took Jesse and the boys on a tour of the outbuildings that housed equipment and tools. Some of what they saw caused Jesse to flash back thirty years. A scythe hung of the wall with a rusty blade. The wooden handles were polished by sweat, and worn smooth by the calluses of his father's hands. The hoes stacked in a corner took Jesse back to long summer days and endless rows of corn and beans. Dust motes drifted lazily in the shafts of sunlight like columns from holes in the roofs.

One building contained an old portable forge unit with a hand crank bellows. Charcoal used to fire the bellows lay in a pile on the floor. Franklin asked Paul to turn the crank. The protesting squeals of disuse made everyone cover their ears. A grindstone bench stood off to one side. One of foot petals was broken off and lay on the floor.

"Let's go check on the horses," Franklin said.

Jesse and the boys followed Franklin to the largest building that passed for a barn in Haven. The strong acrid smell of old musty hay greeted them at the door. A line of pegs along the wall down the right side of the barn was loaded with old leather harness. Pigeons cooed and flew back and forth between the rafters.

Two stall openings were at the far end of the center area. The horses stuck their heads out and looked at the visitors. Their large brown eyes were focused on the men and their ears erect with curiosity at the prospect of something different taking place in their tranquil lives.

"This here's Abby and Fisher," Franklin said. "Fisher is good with the plow and Abby's good for Fisher. I only needed one horse up to now, but Abby's docile and saddle broke."

Jesse rubbed the heads of Abby and Fisher and scratched them behind their ears. He took a hand full of oats from a barrel. Fisher tickled Jesse's hand as the horse's soft lips nibbled the oats from his hand. Jesse looked at the equipment sitting at the far end of the barn. The plow blade gleamed silver from its recent use.

"Franklin, looks to me like you've been working hard around here," Jesse said.

"I did the best I could JJ. We still got a long way to go."

Friends of the Family

"JJ?" Mark asked. "Franklin, why did you call Dad JJ?"

"Never mind about that," Jesse said.

"Why when your Daddy was just a pup, we called him by his initials," Franklin said. "Jesse James Colter. JJ."

"Jesse James Colter? Gees, that sounds like an outlaw or something," Paul said laughing.

"Yeah, Dad. You and mom always said you didn't have a middle name," Mark added.

"Well now you know. It wasn't a name I would have chosen, and your mom used to tease me about it. So I just stopped using it," Jesse said.

"Hey. Not a problem, JJ," Mark said.

"You know what, Mark? I'll just bet that's the last time I'll ever hear that used again," Jesse said. Everyone was smiling, but they knew it would be the last time.

The men stopped by to see the pigpen on the way back to the house. There were two pens with board fences attached. The one pen contained three sows and six baby pigs, running back and forth. The sows lay on their sides and rested in a muddy hole. The baby pigs ran up to the men standing at the fence and stuck little pink flat noses through the fence rails. One of the sows rose ponderously and walked over to the feed trough for the last of the morning's scraps.

"Used to be more baby pigs," Franklin said. "Dogs and such been hitting us real bad. We've lost one every other week or so."

"Something tells me that won't be problem much longer," Jesse said, thinking about Boss.

After the tour, Jessie asked the boys to unload the truck. Sarah gave directions for where to put things. She, Hattie and Lily spent the late afternoon opening up the main cabin, and airing out the bedding and stuffy rooms. As it began to cool towards evening, Jesse and Franklin cleaned old bird nests and leaves out of the chimney and started a fire. They could hear sneezing coming from where the women and Lily were dusting.

They went out onto the large front porch carrying two rockers from inside. Daisy lay on the floor at their feet looking up at them. The sun went behind the west ridge and a blue twilight came quickly.

The men sat and visited for a while. Light spilled out onto the porch as kerosene lamps were lit and set on tables.

"Things been bad around here Jesse. It's getting worse too. Hattie and I don't even go

Friends of the Family

into the Rock anymore. I don't know if you remember them or not, but the Haskins boys has kind a taken over there."

"I remember the Haskins twins. They had a little brother everybody called weasel," Jesse said.

"Well that was thirty years ago. They're men now, and as mean as snakes, killers and cruel, every one of them. They've been raiding places around here, when they feel like it. Mainly robbing, but sometimes taking the women and killing the men. Ain't no law, and nobody's stood up to them. They've left us alone so far, but I think it's only a matter of time," Franklin said.

Jesse thought for a few minutes. He decided that he wouldn't have any secrets with Franklin. He told him about the problems up north with scavengers and about Middletown, the bikers and the girl. He told Franklin about what he remembered about his parents' deaths and his suspicions about how it happened.

"I've decided that no matter what I have to do, Franklin, we're going to survive. When it's time to settle with the Haskins, it won't be pretty. I'll understand if you don't have the stomach for it."

Joel Baker

They sat in silence for a while in the gathering darkness. Jesse knew that Franklin was thinking about what he'd told him. The sounds of the night began to kick in. Whippoorwills called back and forth, crickets sounded at each other, and the frogs by the creek started up. Franklin broke the silence.

"Jesse, I'm just an old black man that's crossed over the street too many times cause some ignorant redneck happened to want to walk where I was. You had it hard, no doubt about it, for the past year or so. It's been hard my whole life. Now I'm closer to the end than the beginning of my life. I have very few years left, and pray to sweet Jesus to forgive my many mistakes. I got reasons for wanting to be a part of what you're suggesting, Jesse, and I got very little to lose. Will I have the stomach for what's got to be done? I believe I will."

"Tell me Franklin, why did you stick by my father all those years ago? I don't have to tell you what a mean cuss he was. Why'd you put up with it?"

"Your papa was a hard man, Jesse, he weren't a mean man. Believe me when I tell you there's a big difference. Far as I could tell he didn't treat me any worse or any better than he did you, your mama, or anyone else. He treated me fair. I never wanted to be treated better than other folk, Jesse. Just wanted to be treated the same."

"You got to know Franklin that I treat situations like the Haskins boys in a particular way. I look at it like a job that's got to be done. I do what I got to do. I don't worry much about what's fair. Let's say you come on a pack of rattlesnakes. You don't get down on your belly and see who can bite who first. You shoot the bastards and move on. Is it fair? Well, the snake probably doesn't think so."

"Yea, verily I say unto you, if you come upon a nest of vipers tread them asunder without thought or consequence," Franklin said.

"What passage of the Bible does that come from?" Jesse asked.

"Why that's from the Book of Franklin, I do believe. Amen," Franklin said.

"Amen," Jesse said.

chapter 17

By the end of the first week in Haven, Sarah had declared war on the wood burning kitchen stove. The large cast iron behemoth had a mind of its own, and Sarah started kicking it every time she walked by. She was convinced the stove hated her, and she felt the same way about the stove. Sarah was considering her options when she heard Lily scream. She rushed for the front porch and found Lily pointing down the east road.

"Mommy, the dogs are hurt terrible," Lilly said.

Sarah saw Boss and the other three dogs walking slowly towards the house. All four appeared injured and bloody. Sarah sent Lily scurrying to fetch Hattie. The dogs limped up on the front porch, dropped to the floor exhausted. Sarah saw Hattie running with a pail of warm water and a cloth sack with her medicines and poultices.

"My Lord, they must have fought a bear," Hattie said, after she reached the front porch.

"Lily, go get your father," Sarah said. "He and Franklin are out with the horses."

Lily took off at a dead run, curls and dress flying. Sarah watched as Hattie bathed Boss gently. He raised his huge head and gave Hattie a lick on the arm and laid his head on the floor. He appeared to Sarah too exhausted to hold it up any longer. Sarah could hear a commotion as Jesse and Franklin raced for the house with Lily in hot pursuit. Jesse was the first to arrive and went to where Hattie tended to Boss.

"It's most peculiar," Hattie said. "Seems to be lots of blood, but I can't tell where it's coming from."

"Same over here," Sarah said, as she quickly checked the other dogs.

"I think I know," Jesse said. "It's not their blood."

Sure enough, after all the blood was cleaned off, they found a nick on one ear and a chew mark on a leg or two, but that was it. Sarah thought that whatever the dogs fought must have paid dearly.

Friends of the Family

"Something tells me I wouldn't want these dogs mad at me," Franklin said, still out of breath from his run to the house.

"Why they're just big old babies," Hattie said. "I think the dogs can sleep over at our place tonight, Franklin. You go put out some water."

***

Daisy had her puppies during the second week in Haven. It was a big event for Lily. The seven little mewing pups snuggled close to their mother. Daisy discouraged anyone but Lily from coming too close. This included the other dogs. Jesse thought it was funny that Boss lay on the porch and appeared to pout. The proud papa couldn't even get close to his own pups.

After a day or two, the pups were much more alert. Two of the pups with strange white markings, had coats that were slightly longer and more curled than the other pups. Sarah remarked that Daisy didn't appear to nurse them, and three mornings later, they found the two pups dead. Jesse buried them by the red cliffs. The remaining pups continued to make rapid progress and all the dogs took a special interest in them.

It was Hattie, and then Jesse, who noticed that the dogs appeared to be training the puppies. They were naturally disciplined. When the pups were five weeks old Jesse noticed they were peculiar in couple of respects. First was their size. They each weighed close to ten pounds as near as Jesse could figure. Second, they always ran everywhere in single file. Jesse would look out the door of the barn, and watch as a row of puppies ran across the yard.

"Strangest thing I ever saw," Jesse said to Sarah that night. "All those puppies moving like that."

"It looks to me like Dr. Frank managed to pull it off. What do you think ever happened to him?" Sarah asked.

"I don't know," Jesse replied. "But if he's looking down on us from heaven, I'll bet he's smiling."

***

"I keep telling you, somebody's been killing my goddamn dogs!" Teddy screamed.

"What the hell are you talking about?" Calvin asked.

Calvin and Clarence were just finishing a huge piece of rancid fat back, with plates of white beans. It'd been raining all morning, and

Friends of the Family

Calvin was developing a bad head cold. To make matters worse they'd run out of whiskey. Clarence was suffering with the shakes after only three days without rot gut and was ready to drink the kerosene out of the lamps. Calvin wasn't in a good mood, and now Weasel was in here whining again.

"I started out with eight dogs. I lost three about a month ago, and three more last night! Only one dragged home, and he was tore to hell too," Teddy whined. "After all the hard training of them dogs I put in and now they're just gone."

"Teddy, that don't even add up right. Besides, most of them were sorry looking, if you ask me," Clarence said. "Except for them three big ones. Them three was the meanest dogs I ever seen."

"Think so do you? Well guess what. They was the first three dogs to come up missing!" Teddy said, visibly shaken.

"You go looking for them?" Calvin asked.

"Yeah. I found them all tore to pieces. Not even worth burying. I did find them studded collars I put on them, but I think a bear got them cause of there was blood everywhere."

"Bear, you say?" Calvin said. "That might be fun to go on a bear hunt. Where bouts did you find them collars?"

"Up by Haskins Hill. Not too far from the old place."

"Isn't that close to where that old darkie Franklin and his wife moved, the old Colter place?" Clarence asked.

"Real close," Calvin said. "Maybe we ought to pay them a visit long as we're in the area. Seems like it's the neighborly thing to do."

"I know something else," Teddy said.

"What?" the twins asked in unison.

"I think more people's living out at the Colter place than just them darkies. I seen tire tracks in the dirt over on Sand Hill road."

Calvin sat with his pig eyes squeezed into slits, suddenly alert. "This is getting interesting. Teddy, how many new people are out there?"

"I don't know."

"You'd better go out and take a look around. Yes sir, I do believe it's time for a bear hunt," Calvin said.

"Are you sure?" Clarence asked. "We don't know who's out there."

"Think about it Clarence. I bet you a hundred dollars they got a stash of moonshine out there," Calvin said.

"Count me in," Clarence replied studying his shaking hands.

Friends of the Family

"Now you're talking," Calvin said.

"Can we run Cassy for bear bait?" Teddy asked. "You know, through the woods until we jump the bear?"

Calvin and Clarence looked at each other. Each waited for the other to speak. Teddy took a big knife out of the sheath on his belt and started rubbing the blade on his filthy pant leg. To Calvin, this was a sure sign Teddy was nervous or agitated. The rain began to fall harder and the wind picked up. Calvin hoped this wasn't the start of a big storm.

"We been meaning to talk to you about her," Calvin said, studying Teddy's reaction. "Strangest damn thing I ever saw. Appears Cassy decided that she'd go be with her family. I went in her room day before yesterday, and found she'd hung herself in that back room. Hung herself with her own dress."

Teddy sat with a dumbfounded look on his face. Whenever he got confused his eyes crossed. Nobody laughed. He looked at his brothers. He calmly put his knife back in its sheath. Calvin thought that was a good sign and broke the silence.

"We better wait a week or so. Make sure we ain't walking into something. Teddy, you go on and ride out to the old Colter place and take a look around."

"Okay, but somebody's going to pay for killing my dogs," Teddy said.

He got up and walked out of the room. Calvin saw Clarence breathe a big sigh of relief. They both knew they'd have to put Teddy out of his misery eventually. They could never agree on when to do it. Calvin thought it would be sooner rather than later.

chapter 18

THE WEATHER TOOK a turn for the worse, and it rained all morning. Jesse and Franklin were sitting on the porch and enjoying a rest from the back-breaking work. Most of the corn and beans were planted. They had a good running start on the huge garden. Jesse and Franklin planned on making a trip up to Linden in the next couple of weeks. Some of the seed they'd put aside had gotten wet and rotted.

All in all, Jesse felt they'd made a really good start. They still needed to plant wheat, oats, and hay on the top part of the valley. Jesse planned on acquiring more horses on their trip to Linden. They needed to fix the wagon first. They needed the wagon so everyone could go, since he wasn't going to leave anyone alone until he solved the Haskin problem.

Jesse had visited Eagle Rock after dark, on several occasions. He'd spotted the Haskin twins in the Shadow Bar and Grill on each visit. He knew where he could find them when it was time to settle up. It was different with Teddy. He was constantly on the move and difficult to locate. Still, it was only a matter of time.

Franklin interrupted Jesse's thoughts. "I been thinking, Jesse, the problem with wild dogs went away since you arrived."

"I thought that might happen," Jesse replied with a smile, as he looked down at the three dogs lying at their feet. He didn't know where Boss, Daisy and the pups were. Sarah had mentioned last night how fortunate it was Hattie and Franklin hadn't owned a dog when they arrived.

"Soon as we finish planting, we need to start cutting timber," Jesse said. "I noticed an old timber mill saw back in the corner of the equipment shed. It appears to still work, but we'll have to sharpen the blade."

"That saw needs a power take-off belt to drive it," Franklin said. "We don't have a tractor that works, or the gas to run it if we did."

"Cole? How much diesel we got in those barrels?" Jesse asked.

Friends of the Family

"I think the tank's about half full, and we have almost a full drum in the back," Cole answered.

"Good. We can rig a belt drive off the truck. Franklin, is the belt in the shed any good?"

"Nothing I can't fix. How you going to use the truck to power that saw?"

"I thought we could take off one of the rear tires, and drive the belt on the rim. We need to cut as many logs as possible first, and pile them close to the saw table so we don't waste gas," Jesse said.

The three dogs on the porch stood and stared up at the East Ridge. The hair running down their backs stood on end. It transformed them into something primeval. Even Jesse was startled by their savage appearance.

The dogs scattered as if they'd heard a starting gun go off. One of the dogs angled off to the right, the other to the left. The third dog made directly toward and up the ridge. Jesse looked back at the small cabin. He saw Daisy racing for the barn with the five pups running as fast as their little legs could pump, single file, behind her.

"Looks like we got company," Jesse said.

***

Teddy watched the group on the front porch for some time. He counted one man, one darkie, and two boys. This was the kind of information Calvin wanted. He watched the small cabin with growing interest. He saw a small girl pass by one of the windows. Teddy grinned when he saw a pretty woman come out on the porch and shake a rug. She'd jiggled a lot in all the right places and Teddy knew the twins would be very interested in that.

He jumped when the dogs sprung from the porch. He'd only gotten a glimpse of the three dogs, but they seemed to be low to the ground, and headed towards him! He ran for the horse he'd tied to a tree on the back of the ridge.

'Son of a bitch! So that's what happened to my dogs,' Teddy thought. The dogs chasing after him were the biggest, meanest-looking dogs he'd ever seen.

Teddy ran as fast as his skinny legs would carry him. When he reached the horse, he vaulted into the saddle, and rode down the far side of the ridge. When he reached the dirt road to Eagle Rock, he whipped the horse as hard as he could. All the way to town Teddy kept looking over his shoulder, sure those dogs would be right behind him.

***

When the dogs made their dash for the ridge, Jesse stood and everyone on the porch stopped talking.

"What was that all about?" Franklin asked.

"I suspect we just got a visit from one or more of the Haskin boys," Jesse answered.

Jesse looked around. Cole and Mark were in plain sight by the oak tree next to the truck. He and Franklin were easy to spot standing on the front porch. Jesse ran over the side yard, and could see Lily through the front window. Sarah came out on the porch and asked Jesse where Daisy and the pups went.

"Sarah, have you been out of the small cabin in the past hour?" Jesse asked.

"Sure. I was shaking rugs. Why? What's wrong?" Sarah asked.

"I'm not sure, but I suspect the Haskin boys were up on the ridge spying on us," Jesse said. "Where's Paul?"

"I sent him to clean the horse stalls first thing this morning. I haven't seen him since," Sarah said, concern showing in her voice.

She and Jesse ran for the barn. It took a moment for Jesse's eyes to adjust to the dark barn. He could hear nothing but rain hitting the roof of the barn, and dripping off the eaves into puddles below. Pigeons cooed softly from high up in the rafters.

"Paul? Paul? Are you in here?" Jesse yelled.

Jesse heard nothing. Then, a head peered over the side of the hayloft above.

"What's up?" Paul asked.

Paul clambered down the ladder and stood between his mother and dad. Sarah grabbed him and held him close.

"Gees, Mom. Why the big fuss? I feel asleep, but I finished cleaning the stalls," Paul said.

"No problem, Paul. How long you been in the barn?" Jesse asked.

"Ever since breakfast; why, what time is it?" Paul asked.

"Never mind that. Come up to the main house. Sarah, you get Hattie and Lily too. Time for a family meeting," Jesse said.

Jesse walked fast towards the main house. Paul was running to keep up with his father's long strides. Jesse gathered Mark, Cole, and Franklin, and all five waited until Hattie, Sarah, and Lily joined them in the front room.

"First of all, you need to know that we may be in for some trouble," Jesse started. "Let me finish and then I'll answer questions. I got bad news and good news. I believe that this morn-

Friends of the Family

ing, one or more of the Haskin brothers were up on the East Ridge, watching us. They were probably scouting us, because they're planning on paying us a visit."

"Can I assume that's the bad news?" Sarah asked.

"Yes. The good news is that Paul was goofing off and fell asleep in the hayloft in the barn. Normally that isn't good news. But as it turns out, whoever was watching us only saw two men and two boys. They will think there are four of us, but there are five."

"What about the women?" Sarah asked.

"Well, they already knew about Hattie, and I think they saw you shaking rugs and Lily in the window," Jesse said.

"What we going to do?" Franklin asked.

"Depends," Jesse said. "Depends on what the Haskin boys do. I haven't heard shots, so that must mean that as soon as they saw the dogs run off the porch, they high-tailed it out of there. I would have. They're too cowardly to try to sneak up on us at night through the woods knowing those dogs are around. I wish they would, but they won't," Jesse said.

"So what will they do?" Sarah asked.

"I expect them to wander in here, tomorrow at the latest. They'll try to get the drop on us. We're going to let them."

"Oh, really nice plan, Jesse...," Sarah said.

"Wait. I'm not done. The three of us were wearing our long coats this morning, thanks to the rain. Franklin, no offense, but they could spot you with or without a coat."

"What? You think I don't know I'm black?" Franklin asked with a smile.

"They are going to come in here in a tomorrow or the next day. They know we know. Paul, Mark, and I are going to wear our long coats for the next few days. When they ride in, they're not going to know about Cole. They're going to think we are all accounted for, right there in front of them. That is going to give us an edge."

What are we suppose to do?" Sarah asked.

"I got to get you out of harm's way. No matter which way this thing goes. You can't stay here". Jesse thought about it for a minute. "I got it! You, Hattie and Lily are going to the shack for the night," Jessie said.

"Oh Lord! I hate that place," Hattie said.

"What's the shack?" Sarah asked.

Franklin and Jesse looked at each other.

"The shack is halfway down the West Ridge. You may have seen it," Jesse said.

Friends of the Family

"You mean that old lopsided shed?" Sarah asked.

"That's it. It's a great place to hide. I'll explain later. You go get some food together and we'll walk up there. I don't know when the Haskin boys will come back for sure, and I want you all safe. You shouldn't have to be there for more than a day."

"What about me?" Cole asked.

"That's where this gets interesting, Cole. Now, they are going to ride in here easy-like. I plan to meet them out front by the oak tree. They know they lost the element of surprise today, when they were spotted up on the ridge. They'll try some small talk, and when they think they have the drop on us, they'll try to kill us."

Jesse looked around the room at the group of glum faces. "I said they would *try* to kill us. Cole, you're going to spend the next day, out of sight, sitting at a shooting stand in the front bedroom window. I guarantee that's not something they will see coming."

Cole started to smile. He saw where this was heading as Jesse continued. "I suspect Calvin will be the one doing all the talking. He always does. Cole, when I say a code word, you're going to blow his head off. Are we clear?"

"What's the code?" Cole asked.

"Blue truck," Jesse replied.

chapter 19

Little Teddy came pounding into Eagle Rock. His horse was lathered and bleeding from the lashing during the hard ride. He slid to a stop outside the bar, jumped off and ran into the back area where his brothers sat at their usual places, cleaning their guns. Teddy was wide-eyed with fear, and breathing hard.

"Jesus, what's wrong with you?" Calvin asked.

"You look like you seen a ghost," Clarence said.

"I just got the shit scared out me, that's all!" Teddy said.

"Calm down and tell us what happened," Calvin said.

"I went out to spy on them people living out at the old Colter place. I was sitting nice as you please for about an hour. Saw everything.

I started to creep a little closer, and all of a sudden, three of the biggest dogs you ever saw, come racing up the ridge, right for me. Man, I thought they had my ass. I ran like crazy, got my horse and rode fast as I could back here. I thought they got me for sure."

Teddy was starting to get his composure back. He looked around.

"Hey, where did you get the hooch?" Teddy asked.

"Never mind that, tell us what you saw," Calvin said.

"Not until you give me some of that, and tell me where you got it," Teddy said.

Calvin poured some of the corn liquor into a jelly glass and handed it to Teddy.

"Some old guy came here first thing this morning. Lives out close by where Cassy used to live. Says he has a still out that way. Wants to give us free shine, if we agree to protect him and his family. Gives us a couple of bottles as a sample," Calvin continued.

"Protect them from what?" Teddy asked.

"Jesus! You dumb as a rock! From us, you asshole!" Clarence yelled.

"You don't gotta scream at me," Teddy said, his feelings hurt.

"Stop yelling at each other, and Teddy, just tell us what you seen," Calvin said.

Friends of the Family

Teddy gave the twins his most malicious grinning leer.

"To start with, I seen the darkie on the porch. His wife must have been in the house. There was three other guys out by the porch too. They was all wearing long brown coats, but I think two of them were just boys," Teddy said. "And there was women."

The twins leaned forward in their chairs, paying closer attention. Teddy took his time pouring a drink and took a slow sip. The twins waited patiently.

"The one is real sweet. She's small and has these pretty little curls," Teddy said as he gazed at the ceiling in silence with a demented look on his face for some time.

"You're killing me. Teddy, I swear to God, you're killing me!" Clarence finally yelled.

"Now Clarence, let Teddy have a chance. Go on Teddy," Calvin said.

Teddy stared at Clarence and pouted.

"Go ahead Teddy," Calvin said in a calm voice.

"Well, there was this real pretty woman that jiggled a lot when she shook the rugs."

The Haskin twins looked at each other, and then back to little Teddy. Calvin knew Teddy was the high priest of back-shooters. He would concede to Teddy's area of expertise.

"What you think we should do, Teddy?" Calvin asked.

Teddy thought about it for few moments, taking slow sips out of his dirty glass of rotgut. The twins waited quietly.

"The way I see it," Teddy said, "is there's one man, two boys and a darkie. All we got to worry about is takin' out the man. Normally, I say we back-shoot him. But, I'm not going near those woods, not with them dogs roaming around up there. No way, I want to tangle with them damn dogs. So, we do like we always do. We just ride in easy-like. Start talking real pleasant like. When Calvin thinks the time's right, we blast the man first, then the boys."

Teddy took his knife out of its sheath and rubbed the edge of it with his thumb. A small red line appeared and blood ran down to his first knuckle.

"Then I say we skin the darkie, and start in on the women," Teddy said.

Calvin thought about it and couldn't find fault with Teddy's plan. He did want to change one little part. Once they were done with the people at the farm, it would be time to fix Teddy. "No sense waiting," Calvin said. "We ride tomorrow morning."

The three Haskin brothers nodded at each other and drained their dirty glasses.

***

Sarah and Hattie hurried around and gathered food into a large wicker basket. They grabbed blankets, some candles, and went back to the big house. Jesse, Paul, Mark and Franklin were waiting for them. All but Franklin were wearing long brown coats.

"Where's Cole at?" Sarah asked.

"Upstairs," Jesse said.

Sarah put the basket down and walked up the stairs. As she entered the small bedroom, Cole lay on the bed with his eyes closed. "Cole, you awake?" Sarah asked.

"Yes, Mrs. Colter," Cole said.

"Cole, I wanted to thank you for coming with us and everything you've done for this family. You're a part of us now. And Cole, you have to know how much we all care about you."

Cole got tears in his eyes. "Thank you," Cole said and rolled over so he faced the wall.

"Cole? Cole, look at me," Sarah said.

Cole rolled back and looked at Sarah.

"You've got a man's job to do tomorrow. But you've been doing a man's job for some time now. I'm entrusting you with the lives of the men I love. I need you to do me one favor?"

"Sure. What's that, Mrs. Colter?"

"Shoot straight," Sarah said, and smiled at him.

"Don't worry, Mrs. Colter. I'll take care of this family."

"I know you will Cole," Sarah said, as she leaned over and kissed him on the forehead.

Sarah came down the stairs and the rest of the group walked out of the house and headed across the fields at the waist of the valley. When they got close to the West Ridge, Jesse turned to Sarah.

"What was that talk you had with Cole back there?"

"Oh, just a little pre-game pep talk," Sarah said.

Sarah looked back at Hattie and Lily as they walked across the field. They were whispering back and forth like good friends. Behind them came Daisy and her row of puppies. Other than an occasional playful nip at the tail in front of them, the puppies maintained good order. They stopped at the bottom of the ridge in front of the shack that rested precariously on the steep ridge wall. They gathered in a group.

"The guys stay here. Girls, follow me," Jesse said.

He started up the steep rocky path leading to the cabin. Sarah, Hattie, Lilly, Daisy, and the puppies followed single file. When Jesse reached the cabin door, he stopped and waited for the women and dogs to join him. Sarah peeked through the door.

"You seriously expect us to spend a night in this shack?" Sarah asked.

"No I don't," Jesse said. "Just follow me, and try to step in the footprints of the person in front of you."

Jesse headed into the cabin. Sarah shrugged and followed him. Jessie walked to the far side of the room, and up to the cabinet against the far wall. He felt along the edge. His fingers touched a small piece of metal about the size of a three-penny nail. He lifted it.

The cabinet swung forward into the room. From behind the cabinet, the mouth of a cave ran off into the dark distance. The air stirred, and blew steadily from the mouth of the cave. Jesse lit a kerosene lamp. He stooped over and disappeared into the cave. Everyone followed in single file.

About fifty yards into the cave, it widened out into a large room. The light from his lantern played off the sides of the rock walls of the cave. The ceiling of the cave disappeared into the darkened heights. In the silence, Sarah could hear dripping water somewhere close, and rushing water in the distance.

Jesse spoke, his voice echoing into the darkness beyond. "Nobody knows about this cave. You'll be safe here. Just make yourselves comfortable as you can. Down that path, about another hundred yards, is a small underground river with water to drink. Make sure you stay on the path. There are side passages that are dangerous. Are there any questions?"

"Oh, a couple of hundred, I guess. Let's start with the obvious one. How did you know about this place?"

"Most people think Haven got its name from the protected valley. But it really got its name during the civil war because of this cave. General Bragg was in charge of keeping the Yankees out of southeastern Tennessee. He had a cavalry unit led by an officer named Morgan. They were called the Morgan Raiders. They operated out of this area even after the Union started pushing the rest of the army towards Atlanta. It was Morgan himself that named this valley Haven. They lived in these caves until they were called down to help defend Atlanta."

"Okay," Sarah said. "Two more questions. Why do people from the south always know so much about the civil war, and just how cold is it in here? I'm freezing."

Jesse laughed. "The answer to the first question is because we don't think it's over. As for the temperature, it's always sixty degrees in here, but you all have blankets. There's some canned food in some of the rooms in case you find yourselves running short. Hattie should know where to find everything. By tomorrow, or the next day at the latest, this will all be over."

Jesse started to leave. "Just a minute," Sarah said. "You don't think you're walking out of here with out a goodbye do you?" Jesse and Sarah embraced and held each other for a few moments.

"I love you, Jesse Colter."

"I love you, Sarah Colter."

Jesse turned and headed into the darkness and the cave entrance.

chapter 20

JESSE LEFT THE cave, re-entering the small dilapidated shack. He closed the cabinet with a snap. As he backed out of the shack, he picked up a piece of sheet metal lying discarded on the ground. He stepped back inside the door and swung the piece of sheet metal back and forth. Dust rose in a thick cloud and slowly settled to the floor. All trace of footprints disappeared.

Jesse climbed back down the side of the ridge. When he reached Franklin and the boys, they saw his jaw set with a terrible resolve.

"Let's go take care of some business," Jesse said, as he continued past them, across the valley.

Franklin hurried to catch up with Jesse. "How'd it go with the women back there in the cave? I bet they weren't too happy about being left there."

Jesse thought for a minute before he replied. "Let me put it this way, not good."

Franklin laughed. I ain't looking forward to hearing Hattie's opinion of being locked in that cave neither."

***

Jesse woke early the next morning and lay in bed, thinking about what lay ahead. Jesse knew, and accepted, the danger. He played it over in his mind. *It was the unexpected that tripped you up*, Jesse thought. *I think I've covered all the bases, I just hope it's enough.*

Before they'd lost all light the previous evening, Jesse had gone upstairs to check on Cole and make sure he was ready. When Jesse sighted Cole's scope he'd noticed a blind spot. It was possible for a man on horse to advance up to the porch and out of Cole's sight.

He'd yelled down for Franklin to saddle Abby, ride out under the oak tree, in front of the porch. He positioned the horse at the limit of the Cole's vision in all four directions. When Franklin reached each point, Jesse told Mark to draw a line in the dirt outside where the horse stood. When all positions were marked, Jesse went downstairs.

"Give me the stick, Mark," Jesse said.
"What are you doing?"
"Just watch."

Jesse took the stick and lengthened the four lines in both directions. When all lines intersected, he stepped back and smiled.

"That's a killing box," Jesse said pointing to the lines in the dirt. "As long as all three riders are in that square, they're ours. Cole, did you hear what I said?"

"I got it," a voice from the upstairs window replied. "If they're in that box, I own them."

They'd decided that Jesse would stand to the front and center of the box. Jesse told Mark to stand to his left and Franklin to stand to his right. They went over the possible things that could happen.

One rider forward, two back. Two forward, one back. All three riders might be in a row. They went over who would do what, and when. All of them agreed that they wouldn't make a move until Cole made his first shot. Jesse would have his shotgun and Mark his sawed off loaded with double OO buckshot. Mark was to pull both triggers and not worry about hitting the horses.

Franklin was a different problem. He didn't know anything about guns and his weapon of choice was a large bowie knife he wore in a sheath. The sheath hung from his belt like a holster and was tied to his leg just above the knee. Franklin refused to learn to shoot and Jesse was reminded of the old joke about the guy who brought a knife to a gunfight, but didn't say anything.

"Are you any good with that thing?" Jesse asked, pointing to the knife.

"Good enough, I believe," Franklin said.

He drew and threw the knife in a single blurring motion, and the knife twanged as it stuck in the oak tree twenty feet away.

"That's way cool!" Paul exclaimed. "Can you teach me to do that?"

"Not by tomorrow morning," Jesse said. "Paul, you're a key part of our plan. You're going to be very important, but I want you to promise to stay by the corner of the porch. At the first sound of a shot from anywhere, I want you to dive under the porch as fast as you can. And I mean fast!"

Paul frowned and looked disappointed. Jesse bent over and looked Paul eye to eye. Jesse put his hands on Paul's thin shoulders.

"Listen Paul to what I'm about to tell you, because it's going to be real important. Tomorrow men are going to die. Not like what you may remember from the movies or television. We're talking blood and guts. Paul, we won't know if it's theirs, or ours, until it's over. Do you understand that?"

"I think so," Paul said. "But what if it's ours?"

"I don't think that's going to happen, Paul. But if it does, you're going to be the last line of defense for Hattie, your mother and sister. So here's what we're going to do. You see this gun?" Jesse asked as he pulled a pistol from the pocket of his coat.

"Yes."

"Well, this pistol's called a Glock twenty six. It will fire every time you pull the trigger. This has a ten round clip. So when all the shooting and yelling is over, anyone sticks his head under that porch that isn't black or wearing a brown long coat, you pull the trigger until you start hearing clicks like this," Jesse said.

Jesse ejected the clip, cleared the chamber, pointed the gun up in the air and pulled the trigger. Paul nodded.

"I'm going to load the gun, and lay it on a piece of cloth under the porch. As soon as you dive under the porch, you scramble over and find the gun. Get your back against the cabin's foundation and stay put. The safety will be off, so don't worry about it. As soon as you're certain that the person looking for you isn't one of us, hold the gun with both hands.

You start pulling that trigger and keep pulling it. Can you remember all of that?"

Paul nodded and stood up straight.

"Fire off some rounds, Paul. Get used to the kick," Jesse said.

Paul fired off a couple of rounds and Jesse reloaded the clip. He placed it under the cabin porch on a towel. Paul crawled under the porch to make sure he could find it in a hurry.

As the sun rose in the valley, Jesse lay in bed worrying about all the things that could go wrong.

What if they don't ride into the box? What if they bring some others? ..Our main edge is their arrogance. We got one more gun than the Haskin boys know about..and we're ready. I've done everything I can. What if something happens to the boys? Why didn't I make Paul stay with the women? Maybe we should have taken them out in Eagle Rock..

Jesse rolled out of bed, put his shoes on, and went upstairs to where Cole lay sleeping. Jesse stood at the door of the bedroom and looked down on the young man. *My God, he's just a kid, barely sixteen. And Mark might be a better choice to be at the bedroom window. Mark could make the shot..and there was*

Cole's hesitation in Middletown when we waited for him to pull the trigger. Besides, I'll be in a better position to protect the boys.. Damn, that's selfish. No, Cole's the one to make the shot..

"Cole, wake up," Jesse said. "You better get yourself some coffee, take care of any business. Then, get to your post."

Cole rolled over. He looked at Jesse and nodded.

"One more thing Cole, we can't afford a hesitation. When you hear me say the words *Blue Truck*, you pull that trigger," Jesse said.

"Mr. Colter? Of all the things you got to worry about this morning? I'm not one of them," Cole said.

"Jesse. You call me Jesse from now on Cole," Jesse smiled, and started down the stairs.

***

Calvin rolled over and sat on the edge of his filthy mattress. The springs protested from the weight sitting on the bed. He scratched himself. Red welts from fleabites covered his body. Blood oozed from some of them, made raw from his long dirty nails. He was naked and gave off an almost visible stench. He looked at his image in the dirty cracked mirror on the back of the door.

He ran his hands through his greasy hair, studying his bulging stomach and the rolls of fat. *Hell, I'm still the best-looking Haskin boy.* He grinned at the grizzled face in the mirror. Brown and yellow teeth surrounded by thick, fat lips, a bulbous, red nose, and fat pig-eyes looked back. *Yep, I definitely got a way with the ladies. Them Haven women are going to find that out today.*

After he got dressed, Calvin walked to the next room and stuck his head in to wake Clarence.

"Wake up you tub of lard!" Calvin yelled. "We're going to go visit our new neighbors."

He went into the Bar and saw Teddy already sitting at the table. Calvin went and started to make coffee. The pail of water was empty.

"Teddy, go fill up this pail," Calvin said.

"Go get it yourself."

Calvin turned towards his little brother and stared. He wore the same blue jeans he'd been wearing for a month. He wore a new white shirt, buttoned to the top, with a bow-string tie. The clasp at the collar was made of brass and looked like the head of a horse. It appeared as though his hair was combed. His cap lay on the table at his elbow.

"What you all dressed up for?" Calvin asked.

"None of your damn business," Teddy replied sullenly.

Clarence came staggering into the room. He was holding his head in both hands as he walked across to the table and sat down next to Teddy.

"I'm begging you, somebody, get me some coffee," Clarence pleaded.

"Can't do it, Clarence," Calvin said. "I'd like to, but little Teddy doesn't want to go get water like his big brother asked. Ain't that so little Teddy?"

"I told you don't call me *little* Teddy no more."

"Well. Well. We all growed up, are we? Looks to be all dressed up too. Guess I'll have to get the water myself," Calvin said, his fat lips pursed.

Calvin picked up the empty pail and started towards the door. When he was even with the table, he threw the pail at Teddy. As the pail hit the table in front of Teddy, Calvin was on Teddy in a heartbeat. He pinned Teddy to the floor with one hand and grabbed the hilt of Teddy's knife. He pulled it and held the blade to Teddy's throat.

"Now you listen you little rat-faced turd, when I tell you to do something you do it! If I ever even think you got a problem with that, I'll gut you like a fish, and make you watch while I do it. We understand each other?" Calvin whispered between clenched teeth.

The knife pressed harder against Teddy's throat. The skin depressed and a thin red line formed. Calvin glared down into his brother's face. Teddy knew he would cut his throat, and not think twice.

Calvin saw the spittle he'd sprayed on Teddy's face. His ham fist tightened on his brother's shirt and he could tell Teddy was having difficulty breathing. Teddy was a hair's breadth from being dead and Calvin knew what would happen next. Teddy always did the same thing when he was really frightened. He wet himself.

Calvin saw the darkness spread down Teddy's pant leg. Teddy started his high girlish giggle. To Calvin it sounded maniacal. The demented giggle had always caused his daddy to stop beating Teddy. It worked this time too. Calvin let go of him as if he'd been shocked by a cattle prod. He stood and picked up the pail.

Friends of the Family

"Now Teddy, you go get the water, so I can make poor sick Clarence a cup of coffee. Then I want you to saddle all of our horses and tie them out front. While you're outside, you clean yourself up," Calvin said in a calm voice.

He dropped the bucket next to Teddy and stuck the knife in the floor between Teddy's legs. Teddy got up and picked up the knife. Calvin watched him closely. Teddy put the knife back in the sheath. He picked up the pail and walked out the door.

"Today's the day for little Teddy," Calvin whispered.

Clarence nodded his head with obvious effort. Two hours later, Calvin thought Clarence was recovered as much as he would. The three brothers walked out to the front of the bar, checked their weapons, mounted their horses, and started towards Haven.

As they passed the light pole in front of the bar, Teddy reached out and gave the feet of Sam Greeley a shove. As the brothers started on the road to Haven, the owner of the Shadow Bar and Grill continued to swing back and forth, back and forth.

chapter 21

It was almost noon, and the sun was directly overhead. Jesse had spent the first part of the morning helping Mark rig a strap for his sawed-off shotgun. They'd put in screws with a long leather strap so that the shotgun would hang loosely under Mark's long coat. Mark practiced bringing it to firing position. They adjusted the strap length several times.

They were now in wait mode. The dogs had disappeared except for Boss. Jesse put the massive dog in the house and locked the screen door. He didn't want the friends, or anything else, to alert the Haskins and put them on their guard. He wanted them over confident. Mark and Paul were by the far left corner of the porch. Jesse and Franklin sat on the front steps. Franklin was whittling a piece of wood with his knife.

Joel Baker

"Looks like we got company," Franklin said, without looking up.

Jesse looked off to the right. On the road in front of the East Ridge, three riders approached at a leisurely pace. Jesse first recognized the twins. He thought the third rider in back must be little Teddy. When the three pulled even with the oak tree, they turned towards some faint lines drawn on the ground. The horses stopped.

Jesse got up and walked to stand in front of Calvin's horse. Mark walked forward and stopped by the dirt lines at the side of Clarence's horse. Franklin kept whittling like nothing unusual was going on.

"Howdy," Jesse said and smiled.

"Well Howdy yourself," Calvin said, with hard eyes and a large grin. "You look familiar. Do I know you?"

"I suspect so, although it's been a few years. Name's Jesse Colter."

"Well, imagine that! We're the Haskin boys. I'm Calvin. You remember my brother Clarence, and my other brother Teddy?" Calvin asked.

"Oh, I remember you, Calvin. I got a broken nose to remember you by. How you been doing?"

Friends of the Family

"Not too good to tell the truth. That's why my brothers and I thought we'd head out this way and see how this darkie," Calvin said, as he waved a hand towards Franklin, "and his new guests been doing."

"Who? Oh, you must mean Franklin here. Franklin, don't you be antisocial, come on over here and say howdy to our guests."

"Yas sir, Master Colter," Franklin said as he stood and walked over to the horses. Franklin took off his hat and held it in both hands as he bobbed his head up and down. His knife was in its sheath. Franklin now stood on the right corner of the faint lines in the dirt.

"I always thought Franklin was a bit uppity," Calvin said. "Looks like you taught him his place, Jesse."

"Franklin knows all about his place. What brings you and your brothers out this way, Calvin?"

"Well, two things really. See, my brother Clarence been feeling poorly, and we figured you'd have just what it takes to fix him up."

"What would that be Calvin?"

"We figure you might have some white lightning. You know the hair of the dog..."

"We got none of that, Calvin. What was the second thing?"

"Why we heard you got women out here. You know. Let us get to know them some. Maybe wax our candles so to speak. We like pretty women," Calvin leered.

"I knew that about you, Calvin," Jesse said smiling like rigor mortis. "By the way, how are your folks? Is your pa still kicking?"

"Naw. That old bastard died a bad way, about five years go. Course he died better than your mama and papa did."

"How so, Calvin?" Jesse asked, his grin fixed like death.

"Oh, I don't know. It was a long time ago. I do remember your Daddy went whining to the law after Clarence and me busted you up some. He shouldn't have done that. Our papa was awful mad."

"Gees, I never knew that Calvin. It does explain some things though."

"Like what?" Calvin asked.

"Like the *blue truck*," Jesse said.

There was a moment, frozen in time. A look of confusion, then comprehension, crossed Calvin's face. The realization that something was seriously wrong registered. Jesse and Calvin locked eyes. Jesse nodded ever so slightly. Calvin's shotgun began to swing off the pommel of his saddle.

Friends of the Family

A rifle cracked. Jesse thought he heard the sound of a baseball bat hitting a watermelon, as Calvin's head exploded and disappeared in a tenth of a second. Parts and bits from their brother's head showered both Clarence and Teddy.

Jesse saw Mark's coat fan outward, as his scattergun swung in a slow arc towards Clarence. Clarence looked dumbfounded at his twin brother who still sat upright in his saddle like the headless horseman. Jesse drew his weapon.

As though moving under water, Clarence shifted his shotgun in Jesse's direction. Jesse fired as Mark pulled both triggers and Clarence was lifted from his horse. In an almost graceful arch, he rose, and then fell towards the ground. He landed on his back with a thud.

Teddy dug his heels into his horse. He was on Jesse before he could react. As he moved forward a knife whistled past his back. Teddy dove filling his hand with the hilt of his knife. He slashed Jesse in midair causing Jesse to drop his gun. As Teddy hit the ground, he rolled to his feet.

Jesse felt the flash of white-hot pain sear the side of his face and shoulder. He knew he was slashed from the cheek to the collar bone.

He dropped to his knees from the force of the blow and fell face-first to the ground. Jesse looked up towards Mark, and knew that Mark was reloading, but didn't have enough time. Franklin ran to retrieve his knife. He saw Teddy reach for his pistol lying on the ground.

In the distance, he heard the crash of a screen door. He saw a black shadow fly over him, and smash into Teddy. He saw Teddy fall forward to the ground towards his pistol.

Jesse blacked out.

Jesse heard voices. He wondered who was making all those moaning sounds. He realized they were coming from him and tried to sit up. Franklin held Jesse and pressed a towel against his shoulder, hard. Jesse felt the flash of pain shoot through the right side of his head. His eyes cleared.

Someone was trying to take his coat off. His head continued to clear. It was Cole. Jesse relaxed and Cole took first his left arm, then his right arm out of the coat. Bone-deep pain racked Jesse's shoulder. He knew Franklin held him, and that he was cutting his shirt off him. He saw his whole right side was soaked with blood.

Mark came out of the house with a pail of water and poured it over Jesse's head and shoulder. The flow of blood slowed, but Franklin continued to press the red towel against his shoulder. The water revived him further. He shook his head.

"Gees, that was fun," Jesse said.

"You okay, Jesse?" Franklin asked.

"I don't know for sure. I'm not sure I even know what happened," Jesse quipped.

"We may have a problem, Dad," Mark said.

"Help me stand up."

Cole and Mark helped him to stand, while Franklin tried to keep the towel on his shoulder. Jesse knew that most of the blood was coming from his face. He saw Paul standing to one side with a worried look, watching him. Jesse surveyed the killing box in front of the porch.

"Mark, get control of those horses before they stomp someone," Jesse said.

Mark collected reins and led the horses off to one side. Calvin had apparently finally lost his balance. His headless corpse lay in the dirt at the center of the square. Clarence was alive and lay towards the back under the oak tree. His head moved slowly back and forth. A small, high keening sound came from him. His chest was a bright red.

Jesse suddenly felt light headed and a bit woozy in his stomach. Cole and Mark grabbed him as his knees buckled. The wave passed and his head cleared again. He looked down at his feet and saw a dog lying on the ground. A knife wound ran the length of the dog's flank and painted it red. It was Boss. His jaws were tightly clamped on Teddy's throat.

Other than having his throat at risk of being ripped open, Teddy seemed undamaged. Jesse noted he had on a silly little string tie with a horse head clasp a small boy might wear.

Jesse watched Boss control Teddy's movements. As long as Teddy remained motionless, the jaws allowed air to pass into Teddy's lungs. If Teddy moved in the slightest, raised a finger, blinked an eye, the jaws tightened. Boss's golden eyes looked up at Jesse. They seemed to ask a question.

"Paul, I want you to go with Franklin up to the shack and let your mom and sister out of the cave." Jesse said.

"Will do," Paul said.

"Franklin, how are you doing?"

"Fine, Jesse."

"Good. Next time we're in a fight with an oak tree, you be sure to bring that knife of yours," Jesse smiled.

"Wasn't my finest hour, was it?" Franklin said, shaking his head.

Friends of the Family

"Hey. Everybody did just fine. Mark, Cole? You guys did great. But we got some cleaning up to do. Paul, give me the gun."

Paul walked to his dad and handed him the gun from under the porch. Jesse checked to make sure the safety was still off and that no rounds had been fired.

"Franklin? You and Paul go up to the cave now. Remember to take your time on the way. Tell Hattie and Sarah that I got a scratch, and I need them to come fix me up. We need some time, so walk slowly."

"Sure Jesse," Franklin said. He and Paul meandered toward the West Ridge and the lop-sided shack.

He watched as the two figures grew smaller as they crossed the fields. When they were some distance away, Jesse walked over to what was left of Calvin. He looked down at the headless torso and moved the right arm over by the torso with the toe of his boot.

"That was for my Dad."

He walked over to the still form of Clarence and knelt down. Clarence stopped moving his head from side to side, and looked up at Jesse.

"Clarence, how are you doing?" Jesse asked.

Clarence started to bawl. He began moving his head back and forth again.

"Clarence? Listen to me. I want you to focus. I want you to look in my eyes," Jesse said, in a quiet, calm voice.

Clarence lay still and looked up at him. Jesse smiled and put the cold barrel of the pistol on Clarence's forehead.

"Good. Now Clarence, I want you to know your brother Calvin's standing before Jesus at this very minute. You and Calvin were always so close. I thought it only right that you go stand with him. This is for my mother, Clarence."

Jesse pulled the trigger. He got slowly to his feet, staggered and regained his balance. He walked over and knelt by Teddy across from where Boss lay. Jesse picked up Teddy's glasses and placed them gently back on him. He noticed the dark stain spreading slowly down Teddy's legs.

"Teddy, I'm worried. Besides the fact you just peed your pants, you got an even worse problem. See Teddy, I can't get these dogs to do anything, unless they want to. Right now Boss appears to want to end your miserable life. The worst part is that I can't think of a single reason why he shouldn't."

Boss's golden eyes never left Jesse for second. They followed his every movement. Jesse looked at Boss and knew this massive dog was the dark shadow that had saved his life. He nodded his head ever so slightly. Boss bit down. He heard the snap and crunch of broken bone and torn cartilage. Jesse thought it was a lot like the sound a dead rabbit made.

Little Teddy's mouth and eyes both opened as wide as a fish, as he died. His arms and legs flailed, twitched, and then lay still. His eyes rolled back in his head as the look of surprise became a fixture. Boss released Teddy's neck, stood and walked over to Jesse. He looked at him, with a look of concern.

"Remember to drag the bodies over under the oak tree and cover them with a tarp, Cole. The women will be here shortly," Jesse said. He toppled forward as he fainted.

chapter 22

JESSE SWAM TOWARD the surface of consciousness. He broke surface and discovered he was heavily bandaged. Sunlight streamed through the windows. Boss was lying on a stack of blankets on the floor next to his bed. Hattie sat next to Boss, gently stroking his head.

"Hey," Jesse said. "Can I get some attention around here?"

Hattie jumped. "Lord! You scared the heck out me! Sarah, Jesse's awake!"

Sarah came into the room and sat on the edge of the bed. She looked concerned and took a hold of Jesse's hand.

"How're you feeling, Honey?"

"Like I've been beat with a baseball bat. How long have I been asleep?"

"A few hours. It's late afternoon. Can you sit up?"

Joel Baker

Jesse sat up and felt dizzy, but his head soon cleared. He actually felt pretty good except he was weak and famished. Sarah helped him out onto the front porch. Jesse sat in a chair and looked around. An ominous tarp covered pile sat in the shade under the oak tree.

Someone had pulled the old wagon out front and was replacing the broken floorboards. They'd removed the left rear wheel and the axle rested on a stump of wood. Jesse could hear the rhythmic ring of hammer on metal coming from the forge shed. He stood and walked carefully down the steps and over to the wagon as Mark and Cole came around the main house.

"Dad, how are you feeling?" Mark asked.

"Better than I deserve. How's the wagon coming?"

"Should have it ready to roll by tomorrow."

"Where are Franklin and Paul?"

"They're out in the forge shed making all that noise."

Jesse straightened and assessed his condition. *I really don't feel too bad. Sore mostly. Next time we definitely need a better plan.* He walked out to where Paul was manning the crank on the forge, and Franklin was driving a rim back on the wagon wheel. Franklin finished and spotted Jesse standing in the door.

"Paul, you can stop turning that crank now, I got the rim back on. Hey, Jesse, about time you got back up and around."

"Maybe Calvin was right. You do sometimes seem a might uppity," Jesse said with a smile.

"You talking big for man bandaged up like a mummy. While you were laying around, I been fixing this wagon. Thought you might want to go to Linden with what's left of the Haskins brothers. If not, you give me the word and I'll gladly dig a hole in the pig pen."

"No. You're doing the right thing. Closest thing we've got for law is Jasper Thiggs. We'll take them to Linden and see what Jasper wants to do about it. I'll be ready tomorrow. Will the wagon be ready?"

"Count on it."

"Where'd you get the rim?"

"I went into town and got one from some junk from behind my old place. I met some folks along the way, Jesse. Told them we took care of the Haskins. Hope you don't mind."

"I don't mind. It was bound to get out in a day or two anyway. Paul, help me up to the house," Jesse said.

Paul came over and Jesse put his arm around him, pretending to need more help than he really needed.

"I remember everything until you and Franklin left, Paul. How did it go for you?" Jesse asked.

"Mom and Hattie were really mad as heck being in that cave and not knowing what was going on," Paul said. "Once they saw you though, they got busy taking care of you and Boss. Mom's real good with a needle and thread. She sewed you both right up."

"Paul, you did a man's job yesterday, and I wanted to tell you how proud I was of you."

"Gees, Dad. All I did was dive for the porch. You guys did all the work."

"You did what I asked you to do, Paul. That's all anyone can expect."

Jesse and Paul walked into the kitchen and Jesse ate a full plate of ham and potatoes with white gravy. Just as Jesse finished, Sarah came into the kitchen, a worried look on her face.

"Jesse, there's a bunch of people walking down the East Ridge road towards the house."

Jesse sent Paul running for Cole and Mark while he walked out on the front porch and sat down in the rocking chair. Boss limped out

Friends of the Family

of the bedroom and followed him out onto the porch. Jesse loaded shells into his shotgun and laid it on the floor by his chair.

As they drew nearer, it looked to Jesse that the group was made up of three men, four women, and about six children ranging in age from two to twelve. Sarah came out on the porch and helped Jesse to his feet as the group entered the shade of the old oak tree and stopped in front of the porch. Jesse noticed that they all stood within the faint lines drawn in the dirt.

"Howdy neighbors," Jesse said.

The oldest man in the group stepped forward, stopped in front of the porch steps, and looked up into Jesse's face.

"My name's Bud Collins, Mr.?"

"Colter. Jesse Colter."

"Well, Mr. Colter, we heard rumors there was a bit of a ruckus out this way this morning. We also heard you took care of it, but was hurt in the process," the old man said.

"News travels fast around here. We did have a little excitement out here now that you mention it. But as for getting hurt, well, we're all just fine."

The old man stared at Jesse's bandaged face and shoulder, and looked confused.

"Oh, you're probably wondering why I'm all bandaged up like this. See I'm learning to use a straight razor and, well long story short, I sneezed and slipped a little. I really don't like using a straight razor," Jesse said smiling.

"Those straight razors can be a might tricky, till you get used to them," Bud said, smiling back.

"As for problems, Bud, I do have few under that tarp right over there. Feel free to take a look, but I'd keep the women and children back if I were you."

Bud walked over and lifted one corner of the tarp and peeked under. He dropped the tarp and walked back over to the porch.

"Mr. Colter, let me be the first to welcome you to Eagle Rock, and express our gratitude for the work you did this morning."

"Call me Jesse. Glad we could take care of it, Bud."

"The women here thought you and your family could use some food, so we brought some covered dishes over just in case."

"Well, that's much appreciated. But only if you all agree to stay and help us eat it."

Introductions were made and people gathered in front of the porch. Bud and Franklin chased some curious youngsters away from the tarp a few times. The women carried dish-

Friends of the Family

es of food into the house after each had introduced herself to Sarah. Many greeted Hattie like old friends.

Lily took the little girls out to see the chickens, and generally took charge of the group. The men gathered around Jesse and Boss on the front porch. They all commented on how Boss was the biggest dog they'd ever seen, but were curious as to how Boss got hurt in the same shaving accident. Pipes were lit and everyone gathered around the rocking chair and talked about weather, livestock, horses, and crops. Everything except what was under the tarp by the old oak tree.

chapter 23

THE NEXT MORNING Jesse slept in. When he was up and dressed, Jesse slowly walked out front and found the Haskin boys in the back of the wagon, covered with the tarp. He went into the kitchen and found Franklin and Hattie with three of the dogs. Boss wasn't one of them.

"Morning. Have you seen Boss?" Jesse asked.

"Morning, Jesse. I saw him out by the creek a little while ago," Franklin said.

Jesse went out the back door and walked towards the creek. The beautiful sunlit morning and blue haze of the valley struck Jesse. He was glad when found Boss lying in the creek soaking his injured side in the cool clear water.

"You think that will help, boy?" Jesse said.

Boss looked up at Jesse and laid his head back in the water. He lapped some water and closed his eyes again. Jesse thought what the heck, stripped naked, and waded into the creek. The water was bone-jarring cold. Jesse sat, then laid flat in the fast-running water and let the creek do its work. After several minutes, Jesse climbed out of the creek and dried off as best he could, and pulled his pants on. He took the bandages off his face and shoulder. When he looked towards the house, Sarah was walking towards him through the tall grass. Jesse appreciated her beauty and grace.

"I brought you a small mirror," Sarah said. "I thought you might want to see what kind of a seamstress I am."

"I was kind of curious to know how bad my face's going to be. I just hope I don't look like a quilt or something," Jesse said.

He took the mirror and examined his face closely.

"You got to be kidding! Are you going to be able stand me sitting across from the table from you?" Jesse asked.

"Just for the next thirty or forty years," Sarah said. "Besides, once it heals, I think you'll just have a little white line."

Sarah sat for a minute before continuing. "Jesse, I was so frightened sitting in that cave.

Friends of the Family

If anything had happened to you or the boys I don't know what I would have done."

She started to cry softly and Jesse took her in his arms. "Sweetheart, don't cry. I needed to know that you were safe. I don't think I could have focused if I had to worry about you, especially in your condition."

"I know Jesse, but I'll never do it again. You teach me to shoot or whatever you have to do, because I'll never be anywhere but by your side from now on," Sarah said.

Jesse and Sarah sat on the edge of creek and held each other's hand. They watched Boss lay in the cool clear water. After a while Hattie and Franklin walked out to the bank of the creek next to them. Hattie took off her shoes rolled up her pant legs and waded into the creek by Boss. She rubbed his head and talked softly to him. Boss looked up into Hattie's eyes.

Finally he stood and walked up onto the bank and shook, sending water all over everybody. They laughed and ran, but returned to examine Boss's injured side. Sarah and Hattie both thought it was healing nicely.

Franklin and Cole harnessed Fisher up to the wagon and saddled Abby for Jesse to ride to Linden. They tied the three Haskin horses to the back of the wagon. After Jesse ate some biscuits and gravy, they mounted. Cole climbed up next to Franklin in the wagon. The rest of the family was standing in the yard saying goodbye, when a lone horseman rode down the East Ridge road. It was Bud Collins.

"Morning, everybody. I thought I heard you say you were going to take the Haskin boys to Linden today. If it's all right with you, I thought I'd ride along. Thought maybe Jasper Thiggs should hear just exactly some of the things those three have done around here," Bud said.

"I appreciate that Bud," Jesse said.

Jesse looked down at Sarah. "We better get going. It will be after dark before we get back, so I don't want you to worry."

Just as they were beginning to pull out, Franklin stopped the wagon. "Looks like we got others that want to go along," Franklin said. Three dogs came running across the porch and jumped in the back of the wagon and lay down on the top of the tarp.

"Damn!" Bud said. "Sorry Mrs. Colter. Jesse, I thought that one monster was the only dog you owned. These dogs are almost as big."

"That's true, Bud," Jesse said. "But they're not our dogs. They're just friends of the family."

Friends of the Family

The four men, six horses, three dogs, one wagon, and the Haskin brothers headed down the East Ridge road and turned towards Linden. They traveled on dirt roads except for the last three miles. Franklin had to drive the wagon down the shoulder because the sound of the steel rims on the pavement made the dogs uncomfortable and raised a racket. When they got to the outskirts of Linden, they decided to go directly into town.

They passed a dead stoplight that still hung over the street. Franklin pulled the wagon to a stop by the curb in front of the general store. He climbed down, and tied Fisher to the parking meter.

"Anybody got change for the meter?" Franklin asked.

Everybody was still laughing when Jasper Thiggs and his son Luther walked out of a coffee shop a few doors down the street from where they stood. Jasper walked up to Jesse and the wagon sitting outside the general store.

"Jasper, I don't know if you remember me, but I'm Jesse Colter, from Eagle Rock. These two are my friends Franklin Pierce and Bud Collins. That boy is Cole."

"Heck, I remember you and you all appear to be in a good mood. What the hell happened to your face Jesse? Is that blood I see on your shirt?" Jasper asked with obvious concern.

Jesse looked at his shoulder and sure enough he'd sprung a leak somewhere between Haven and Linden. Jesse undid a couple of buttons on his shirt and peered under. The stitches were in place, but blood was soaking through the bandages.

"Well, Jasper that's why we came to see you. We had a little dust up down our way yesterday."

"A little dust up you say? What does the other guy look like?"

"Take a look for yourself. They're in the back of the wagon, under the tarp."

"I will once you get those dogs out of there," Jasper said, pointing to the dogs sitting in the back of the wagon.

"Cole, see if you can get those dogs to follow you across the street," Jesse said.

Cole walked over to the back of the wagon and lowered the tailgate.

"Not sure it's going to work, but here goes. Come here dogs!" Cole yelled.

The dogs looked at Cole patting his leg as he backed across the street, then back at Jesse. Jesse motioned with his head and the dogs jumped down and followed Cole. Jas-

Friends of the Family

per walked to the back of the wagon, lowered the tailgate and lifted the tarp by one corner. After a good look, Jasper let go of the tarp and raised the tailgate on the wagon.

"I recognize Clarence and Teddy, and judging by the size of the other one, I'm guessing Calvin. You want to tell me what happened to the Haskins?" Jasper asked.

Between Bud and Jesse most of the story came out. Even Jesse didn't know everything the Haskin brothers had done to the people of Eagle Rock. Jesse ended the story with the day the three brothers rode in and most of what transpired. Jasper listened patiently until Bud and Jesse finished.

"What about you Franklin? You got anything to add?" Jasper asked.

"No. I think they covered it pretty well. I can tell you stories of what the Haskin boys and their old man did over the years to black folk, but it's in line with what they told you," Franklin said.

"I think I got the picture, Jasper said. "I would like to hear some specifics about how those Haskin boys died. Now Clarence appears to have been cut in half with a sawed-off shotgun and Calvin looks like he took a head shot from close range from a high-powered rifle," Jasper said as he looked across the street to where Cole stood.

"What I don't understand is how Teddy bought it? I wonder who or what could have damn near decapitated him like that?"

Jesse looked Jasper in the eye. "Those details are a little fuzzy. But I can tell you that I'm responsible for everything that happened. And Jasper, I'd really appreciate it if that was where you left it."

"Okay, I will. But I got to tell you Jesse, I'm disappointed in you. You never struck me as someone who would take credit for another man's good works."

Jesse looked confused and then it dawned on him where Jasper was going with this and he smiled.

"In all my days, I never knew three men that needed killing worse than those Haskin boys," Jasper said. "Now if you want to have Franklin run that wagon out to the ravine north of town, we'll be well rid of them. We can go have a cup of coffee and relax," Jasper said.

"Franklin and I go everywhere together," Jesse said. "I hope that's not a problem in this town."

"Franklin's always welcomed in Linden," Jasper said.

Friends of the Family

"Glad to hear it," Jesse said. "Cole, make that dump run north of town and then look us up. Bud would you give Cole a hand?"

"Sure Jesse. No problem," Bud said.

"Thanks. Jasper, what should we do with the Haskin horses?"

"Sell them or keep them, Jesse, that's up to you. Now let's go have some coffee and pie. I got one more thing to say though before we go anywhere. You keep those bears you call dogs close to you. I like my neck just the way it is," Jasper said.

The three men walked down to the diner, scraped their shoes off, and entered the small eatery. Ten tables covered with red and white checked tablecloths sat in front of a long counter. Jasper chose a table towards the front just as a heavyset woman came out of the kitchen door wearing an apron covered in white flour.

"Jesse, my wife, Betty. Betty this here's Jesse Colter and his friend Franklin."

After the introductions, Betty brought out heavy coffee mugs and matching plates with large wedges of Blueberry pie. The men visited for awhile about the weather and things in general as they finished their pie.

"How do you explain Linden?" Jesse asked. "We came nearly four hundred miles to get here, and Linden was the first town we saw that looked like it was still a community."

Jasper thought for minute before answering. "It helped that I was already the county sheriff, Jesse. When the refugees from up north starting arriving, and the phones, electricity and everything else stopped working, people kind of looked to me for answers. We made it up as we went along. Some of it involved frontier justice like you went through yesterday."

"When we first got here, a market was set up in the middle of the street," Jesse said. "How do people pay for stuff?"

"Barter mostly. Let's say you got a chicken and I got some coal oil or a pie or something. Well if I want that chicken, we negotiate until we decide to trade. Takes a while to figure out, but you'll get the hang of it. You find out real quick what has value, and what's just old stuff nobody wants anymore. There's a lot of that."

"Jasper, do you have any idea where all the people from up north went? We came from southwest Ohio after hard winter, and it was almost deserted by the time we left. With no TV or radio, we couldn't even find out what was going on," Jesse said.

"I'm not real sure. We heard rumors from people passing through. God only knows how many people died. We had long lines of people filing through here for months. Lots of them were sick. But mostly, it seemed to me like some people just ran out of grit. Broke your heart it did, especially if they had little ones. But, nothing we could do. We just kept saying there was nothing here and to keep moving to those poor souls."

"Where were they all headed?" Jesse asked.

"Mostly they were heading south and west. A lot them were looking for relatives. I suspect those with some family and spunk, are homesteading some place and surviving on guts and determination. There wasn't much of that around towards the end. Some people just gave up. Those are the lumps of clothing you see in cars by the side of the road."

Cole and Bud walked in and got their coffee and pie. They sat down at the table next to the men. Jasper studied Cole closely.

"Cole, how old are you?" Jasper asked.

"I turned seventeen about three weeks ago," Cole answered.

"Well, you strike me as someone that can handle himself. You ever think about becoming a law man?"

"Well if I can get another slice of this pie, I would seriously consider it," Cole smiled.

"I thought that in a year or two, you might want to come up here to Linden and work with my son Luther and me for a few months and take it up as a trade. We're going to need strong honest men that aren't afraid to pull a trigger if need be. Judging from your Daddy here, it runs in the family," Jasper said.

Jesse and Cole looked at each other and smiled.

"All three of my boys are straight and strong," Jesse said. "What do you think, Cole?"

"I think that would be very interesting," Cole said.

"I know we're going to need somebody in Eagle Rock about that time Cole," Bud said. "Maybe you could come back to the Rock and look after us when Jasper's through with you up here."

"I think we got us a plan," Jasper said.

"Well we got to be heading back home or Franklin and I will be sleeping in the barn," Jesse said.

"Spent a few nights there myself," Jasper said smiling.

"Good chance you'll be there tonight," Betty yelled from the kitchen.

"Woman's got ears that can hear anything," Jasper whispered.

Friends of the Family

When everyone was mounted and ready to head out, Jesse rode over to where Jasper and Betty stood.

"Jasper, thanks for everything. Betty, the pie was wonderful, and if my wife Sarah can just get the bread to rise, we'll bring some to trade for your pie the next time we're up here."

"Don't you worry about it, Jesse," Betty said. "You just make sure that the next time you come, you bring that wife of yours with you. Franklin, you make sure your wife comes too."

The small procession headed towards Haven. It was well after dark when they came down East Ridge road and saw the cabins with light streaming from the windows. Sarah and Hattie sat in the rockers on the front porch. Mark, Paul and Lily sat on the steps. Boss and Daisy were there, with their puppies sitting beside them, in a row.

Jesse stopped Abby to admire the scene and wait for the wagon to catch up. *What a beautiful sight. This is where we should be. It's good to be home!*

chapter 24

Jesse healed slowly over the next month. Franklin showed the boys how to harness a team of horses, and the difference between gee and haw. Jesse supervised the conversion of the truck into a power takeoff for the logging saw. Cole and Mark were put to work felling trees with trunks that were a foot in diameter, and sixteen to twenty feet in length. The ringing of axes and the sound of crosscut saws resounded off the sides of the ridges.

They used logging chains and Fisher to drag the logs down to the saw. Jesse and Franklin repaired the takeoff belt and mounted it on the rear axle of the truck. When they were ready Franklin and the boys hoisted one of the logs up onto the rollers of the cutting table. Jesse fired up the truck and the belt turned freely.

"Paul, you climb up in the cab and give it some gas when it starts cutting," Jesse said.

The dogs sat side by side on the porch watching with apparent interest. Jesse yelled to Franklin to engage the blade and Franklin grabbed the large lever and pulled it towards him. The saw blade started to spin slowly and picked up speed until it was humming at a high whine.

"Mark, start feeding the log, slowly," Jesse said.

Mark started the log forward. The first cuts were intended to square the log and remove the bark. When wood met the steel blade the resulting scream sent the dogs running in all directions. After the first cut, they rolled the log back and rotated it a quarter turn and repeated the process. It took ten minutes to square the first log. After four passes, the beam was a solid square, nine inches on a side.

They shut the truck down. The women came out on the front porch. The men stood around admiring their first squared timber. Franklin and Mark were both covered with sawdust from head to foot. The sweet smell of fresh-cut wood hung in the air. All the men shook hands and slapped each other on the back with congratulations. There were high-fives and at least two chest-bumps in celebration.

"You men," Hattie finally said with some disgust. "You just cut the log, you didn't make the tree." Everyone looked as Hattie disappeared back into the house, and started laughing.

"See what I got to put up with?" Franklin said, with some pride.

"I heard that Franklin Pierce!" Hattie yelled from inside the house. Franklin bowed his head in defeat, but was laughing along with everyone else.

Jesse gave Paul the job of dragging the scraps from the squaring process down to a shed and piling them for later use. As the sawdust formed a small mountain, Jesse decided to save it as well; Paul was given a wheelbarrow and shovel.

That night Jesse sat down with some pencils and paper, and did some figuring. He felt that with the trees available, providing timbers and boards for Haven would be important. Excess lumber could be used to trade for whatever else they would need over time.

Jesse was confident they could sustain themselves based on the food raised in Haven. But they would need something of value to meet their other needs. Timber was a good possibility, except for one problem. From what they'd got done today, Jesse calculated that their fuel for the truck would be gone before they cut enough timber to build up Haven, let alone have extra for trading.

"Paul, run next door and see if Franklin can come over. Find Mark and tell him to come in here too," Jesse said.

Paul shot out the door. Franklin and Mark came back a few minutes later with Paul, and all three sat down around the table next to Jesse. Jesse told them his ideas about a lumbering operation and the need to come up with a permanent power source to drive the saw.

"OK guys, here's the deal. We need a way to drive that saw after we run out of diesel fuel. If we don't find a way to drive it, someone's going to be in the hole," Jesse said.

"What do you mean?" Mark asked.

"Before people used power saws, they used a cross cut pit," Jesse explained. "You laid a timber or log across a pit about eight feet deep. One guy crawled into the pit and one stayed up with the log. They'd start the crosscut saw with one pulling and the other pushing. They would adjust the log across the pit until they'd cut the full length."

Friends of the Family

"It was really bad up top, but nobody wanted to be in the hole. It was hot, tiring, and dirty work," Franklin added.

"So I need everybody to think about how we're going to power that saw. Let's brainstorm a little," Jesse said.

Everyone sat for a while and looked around the room and at each other with blank stares. Jesse thought that this was going nowhere fast.

"Let me start," Jesse said. "If we could get our hands on a boiler or steam engine, we might be able to make that work. In fact that would be best. You could use coal and in a pinch wood scraps to heat the boiler. Anybody know where we could get a steam engine?"

Nobody did. Paul was deep in thought while Mark and Franklin looked at the ceiling and the floor. Paul's face lit up with an idea.

"Dad, what if we rigged a crank like we use for the fan for the forge?"

"Well, we would have a hard time keeping a saw blade spinning, but good idea," Jesse said, thinking it over. "Wait a minute! Paul may be on to something."

Everybody looked first at Paul, and then Jesse.

"Franklin, that creek's deep and fast," Jesse said. "The principle behind a water wheel is that it turns slowly, but consistently. If you connect a small wheel to a large wheel with a drive belt, the small wheel spins many times faster than the big wheel."

Both Franklin and Mark looked confused.

"Look. If a wheel, twenty feet around, completes six complete revolutions per minute, how many feet would a belt advance in that minute?" Jesse asked.

More confused looks came from Franklin and Mark.

"One hundred and twenty?" Paul ventured.

"Bingo. Now if we hooked a belt onto the saw drive hub that's one foot in diameter, how fast would the saw turn?"

"Same answer. One hundred and twenty," Paul said.

"Correct. Now, double the speed of the big wheel and how fast is the saw spinning?"

"Two hundred forty turns a minute," Paul answered.

"If you two don't mind, Franklin and I are going to leave," Mark said. "We're getting a headache listening to you two."

As they left, Paul moved over by his dad and they began drawing pictures and planning how a water wheel could be constructed capable of driving a saw blade through timbers. They worked late that evening and Jesse went to bed thinking about flywheels and transfer vectors. Jesse was truly happy.

***

Sarah lay in bed next to Jesse, listening to his excitement over Paul's mechanical aptitude and getting started on the water wheel. Sarah placed her hand on her stomach and felt a hard little ball. She smiled to herself as she sensed growing life. She fell asleep thinking of names. *Jessica*, she thought. *I've always loved the name Jessica.*

***

The next morning Cole, Mark, Franklin and Paul joined Jesse on the front steps.

"We've got to get organized," Jesse said. "The garden's in, but we have to get started on the corn, hay, wheat, and oats in the north side of the valley. Franklin, what do you need to make that happen?"

"I think Mark and I can handle the plowing, dragging, and harrow work. But we'll need help with the planting. With Fisher and that other big horse, we should be ready to plant in a week or so."

"Did you say *'That other big horse'*? We got to come up with better names," Jesse said with a chuckle.

"Well, Mark and I actually did come up with names for the horses, but we weren't sure what you'd think," Franklin answered.

"What were they?" Jesse asked.

"We named the big ones Calvin and Clarence and the little one Teddy."

"You and Mark take Fisher and.., Calvin out and get started. As for the names, I couldn't come up with better names than those three horse's asses. The names will remind us to stay alert," Jesse said.

"Amen to that," Franklin said.

"Cole, I need you to scout out the area around Haven. If you find people living anywhere around here, you watch them. When you think it's safe, introduce yourself. If we got another nest like the Haskin brothers nearby, I want to know it first. Decent folk we'll want to meet and get to know. Keep track of anything that might be of use to us that looks abandoned. We're interested in everything, but especially steam engines, boilers, and old farm equipment. Ride Clarence, and if you can get one of the dogs to go, take one of the friends with you."

Friends of the Family

"What you going to be doing Dad?" Mark asked.

"Paul and I are going to build a water wheel. Franklin, we still got all those acetylene tanks from the truck?" Jesse asked.

"Sure do. Why?" Franklin asked.

"Cause I need those tanks to weld metal plates from the truck for the paddles on our new water wheel," Jesse said.

chapter 25

THE NEXT SIX MONTHS brought big changes to the valley. Paul helped his dad, and Lily hung on every word Hattie said. Hattie knew a lot about folk medicine and Lily soaked it up like a sponge. They would go on long walks on the ridges.

"Just remember that every plant I'm going to show you has good effects. We group them as either for sickness or wounds. Some, believe it or not, are good for both," Hattie told Lily. "For right now, just remember which is good for what."

"Okay."

Hattie leaned over and picked up a small leafy plant growing next to a fallen log.

"Now this here's called Feverfew. You can tell it by its fine feather petals. Can you guess what it's good for?" Hattie asked, as she bent over the frail plant.

"Fevers?"

"Yes, fevers, but it's good for those that get real bad headaches too. When someone chews it though they got to be careful to just chew a little, or it will give them mouth sores."

Hattie walked a few steps over by some ferns and picked up another plant.

"Now this plant with the odd-looking pods is called Skullcap. An old Cherokee woman told me about this, when I was just a little girl your age. You make a tea drink using the pod once it's been dried and ground up. It's good for calming your nerves and digestion. It's real good if you're having a particular hard time of the month. Has your mama told you about that yet?" Hattie asked.

"No," Lily said, looking confused.

"You got time so don't you worry about it," Hattie said. "Well looky here! See this pretty yellow flower? That's called Marigold. It's a really good plant God gave us. Now this is one of those plants that can be used inside or out. You pick the flowers like this. Lily, you need a whole bunch of them. You put just the flowers in a wood bowl and you smash them until they give up their oil. It becomes a kind of paste. That paste's good for burns, infections, and all sorts of things when it's spread on the skin. You just eat the dried petals and it will help cure a stomachache or inflammations. Best of all, the flowers are so pretty, these we plant up around the house just to look at."

Lily paid close attention to everything Hattie said. She learned to identify over sixty plants in Haven alone that could be used for different ailments. Hattie would test her by pretending to be ill.

"Oh, Lily, I got a terrible case of the trots. Go find me something to ease my suffering," Hattie would say, rolling her eyes back in her head.

Lily would tear out of the house and up into the woods. She would head for a particular place where she could find an abundance of Slippery Elm. She'd find some dry bark, race back to the house, and make up a strong cup of tea from the bark. Very carefully she would carry the cup of tea and some of the bark to Hattie, who would be waiting on the porch.

"Let's see what you got here," Hattie said.

She would examine everything and if it appeared right, she'd drink the tea and give Lily a big smile. Neighbors would stop by with various ailments, and Hattie would take the neighbor aside so they could talk in private.

"Just a second," Hattie would say. "I have to get my assistant to help me."

Lily would come over and listen to what was said. Hattie would confer with Lily like a consulting physician.

"What do you think Lily?" Hattie asked.

"What about Shepherd's Purse?"

"Well, yes. It will help if she drinks it as a tea during delivery," Hattie said. "Go get several pods for the neighbor."

Lily quickly became generally known as a healer. If Hattie were busy or gone, people would ask for Lily's advice. It wasn't long before Lily was in much demand.

The pace of life slowed to match the rhythm of the seasons. At first the changes came in small steps. Sarah blossomed, as baby Jessica grew within her.

The water wheel was located close to the limestone ledge where the water gushed out of the ground. Jesse used the steel from old power line towers for the superstructure and the metal plates from the truck for paddles. They lifted the completed assembly into place using the last of the diesel fuel with the truck. At the source, the flow rate of the creek was steady and strong. They were able to not only drive the saw when needed, but a grinding stone for milling grain when the saw was idle.

Friends of the Family

Cole spent days away from Haven, roaming the area around the isolated valley. He possessed a real talent for salvage and was able to create a mental inventory of where things could be found. Eventually, things just got too numerous to remember and Cole began writing down everything in logs. He then hid the books where no one but he could find them.

The crown jewel of his searches was a vintage, coal-fired steam engine, he found in a storage hut at the old TVA facility at Basking Ridge. It was buried under a pile of old iron rods and wooden crates. If it had not been marked Kramer Steam Engine on the side, Cole wouldn't even have known what it was. It took a full week and all of Franklin's skill with horses to transport the engine on a low slung wagon pulled by twelve plow horses borrowed from neighbors. They built a special shed to house it some distance from the cabins, using the stack of lumber that was growing in the curing barn.

Mark took on the lumbering operation that moved steadily away from the east and west ridges surrounding Haven. A mountain of logs began to grow close to the site of the water wheel as the truck fuel dwindled ever lower. The voracious appetite for wood consumed by the wood stoves, fireplaces, and cook stoves kept Mark busy as fall and winter approached.

Franklin borrowed time from everyone to help with planting and weeding the gardens in the south end of the valley, and hay and grain ripening in the north end. Lily and Hattie made their trips into the woods to collect their medicines only after they finished the washing, cleaning, cooking, and tending the huge garden.

It didn't help that Sarah was having a difficult time with her pregnancy. Jessica was going to be a Christmas baby. When Sarah started to have pains in the middle of October, she took to her bed. Hattie handled the care and feeding of the tired crew, when they dragged in for meals, and fell into bed at night. Tempers flared on occasion, and everyone was approaching exhaustion. Finally, the harvest was done and the leaves, turning the yellow gold of autumn, fell from the trees.

***

Jesse waited for Cole to return from one of his scouting trips and called a family meeting. It was a cold and gray morning in early November. Everyone gathered in the front room. Jesse stood in front of them.

Friends of the Family

"We've been in Haven for seven months, and it feels like seven years to me," Jesse started. "Sarah's not feeling well, Hattie and Franklin look exhausted, and I can guarantee you, I am. Paul and Lily haven't picked up a book since we got here. We have to butcher some of our pigs, and get ready for the horses to foal in the spring and then start all over. I'm open to suggestions, people. Anybody got something they want to say?"

"I think we need to pick and choose better how we spend our time," Franklin said. "I think the water wheel you and Paul come up with is a fine idea. But we got other fish to fry first."

"Well Franklin, we got enough grain and hay to feed an army, and whose idea was it to plant tomatoes in half the garden? Dad, you promised us no more tomatoes after Ohio," Mark said.

"Why don't you give that axe a rest, Mark and styop chopping down every tree in the valley?" Hattie asked. "We don't need more logs we can't cut up. You might want to wait until we got something we can cut them with. Place is starting to look like a stump farm anyway."

Sarah, sitting sprawled on the sofa looking uncomfortable and concerned, finally spoke.

"Okay everybody, we got a few kinks to work out of Jesse's otherwise perfect plan. But let's not forget everybody's doing the best they can. We're all exhausted and need to back off a little. Everything we're trying to accomplish is important to Haven in the long term, even Jesse's windmill."

"Water wheel," Jesse corrected.

"Whatever! We need to get everything done and we're only missing one thing. Hands," Sarah said.

"I have an idea," Cole said. "I've met some people. I think they're good people having a tough go of it. The main problem appears to be bad land and bad planning. I could talk to some of them and see if they would be interested in moving closer."

Everyone looked at Cole.

"What people?" Sarah asked.

"There's the Scroggins family for one. They live on a rock pile they call a farm about halfway to Basking Ridge. They're really nice and have a boy about Paul's age and a girl about Lily's age. Oh, and little twin babies."

"Anybody else you can think of?"

"...then there's Karen. Her mother died about three months ago and she's been living alone ever since. Karen's got a dog she's fond of but I told her about our friends and how other dogs don't do well around them. She's about my age and…"

"Well, well," Hattie said with a smile. "That explains why Cole's trips been taking longer and longer I do believe."

"Aw Hattie, you always got to make a big deal out of everything," Cole said.

"Please people, focus," Sarah said. "Cole? Why don't you talk to Karen and see if she would like to have a place to live. Franklin? Hattie? You have an extra bedroom. Would you be willing to let Karen stay there?"

"If she can help out around here, she's more than welcome."

"Good. Cole, is this Scroggins fellow handy at all?"

"He appears to be. Keeps his place real fixed up and sure knows his way around horses and livestock. They seem like decent folks and real hard working."

"That sounds good, Cole. Why don't you invite them over for a visit? Jesse, you check with Bud or Jasper to see if they've heard of them, and we'll decide when they get here. As for the rest of us, let's all try to remember where we were just a short time ago, and try to keep a little perspective. Jesse? Anything you want to add?"

"Nope. I think you covered it just fine. But it's a water wheel, not a windmill."

Everybody laughed at Jesse's hurt look, until even he smiled.

chapter 26

Cole left the next day, taking two extra horses with him. Three days later he and a pretty young woman came riding down East Ridge road. She had all her earthly possessions on the third horse. It wasn't much. Everyone ran out onto the porch and watched them ride up. Karen was as tall as Sarah, and very thin. Her long dark brown hair was pulled back and tied with a yellow scarf.

"She's seems nice, Mom," Lily said.

"Hush, Lily. Let's wait until we get to know her," Sarah whispered.

The two climbed down off the horses and Cole introduced everybody. Sarah noticed that from the way Cole and Karen glanced at each other, chemistry was at work here. They moved Karen into the spare bedroom at Franklin and Hattie's place and learned over

Joel Baker

the next few weeks that not only was she a good worker, but she a good person as well.

Hattie commented at dinner one night, that Cole's trips didn't seem to last quite as long as they used too. Both Karen and Cole blushed and smiled at each other. It was obvious to everyone at the table that Cole and Karen were growing more than fond of each other. Jesse made a mental note to check with Bud on the progress on the new church in Eagle Rock.

The Scroggins were invited over for Thanksgiving. Sarah had been virtually bedridden for some time. Her condition was not getting better. For a week before the big day, Hattie and Karen cooked nonstop. A dusting of snow arrived the day before Thanksgiving and the guests were expected that afternoon. The smells coming from the kitchen were driving everyone crazy. Hattie and Karen took turns shooing everyone out of the kitchen. It was a full-time job defending the cakes, pies, and hams being slowly cooked in the wood stove. Hattie thought Karen was a little slow getting Cole out from under foot.

"They're here!" Paul yelled as he came tearing through the house.

Dogs and people scurried to line up on the front porch to see the Scroggins arrive. It

Friends of the Family

was spitting snow and the wind was whipping in gusts. Four horses with riders, and a black and white cow, walked down the road by the trees that marked the sharp rise of East Ridge. The last rider led the cow by a tether.

The riders were bundled against the cold and it was hard to determine who was who. They stopped under the oak tree and the tallest figure carrying a baby bundled in blankets dismounted and stood by his horse.

"My name's Sam Scroggins. Would you be the Colter's?" he said.

"Welcome. My name's Jesse."

"Excuse me for asking, but you got those wicked-looking dogs under control?" Sam said, looking at the dogs on the porch. "Cole told us about a *'no dog rule'* at your place."

"Well, that's a good question. Control may be a bit too strong a word, but you and your family got nothing to worry about from our friends. It's a long story, and I'll explain later. Let's get into where it's warm," Jesse said.

Jesse introduced everybody once they were all inside. Sam introduced his family. There was his wife Mary, oldest son Eddie, their daughter Peg, and the twins Zack and Zeke. Sarah and Hattie made a rush for the babies the Scroggins carried in their arms.

"Their full names are Zachary and Ezekiel," Mary said proudly.

The two baby boys were about four months old and very chubby, unlike the rest of the Scroggins, who were blade thin. When Mary smelled the aroma of the food cooking in the kitchen, Sarah thought she might faint.

"Why don't you and the kids come into the kitchen, while the men look after the horses and that cow," Sarah said.

Sarah held one of the babies tightly as they entered the kitchen.

***

The men went outside and led the horses and cow to the barn, bedded them down, and filled the feeder racks with hay for them.

"That's a fine looking milk cow," Franklin said. "Seems a might skinny though."

"That's why I brought her. Cole said you had plenty of hay and grain. To put it bluntly, we don't have enough for the horses, let alone a cow. I would appreciate it if you would take her as a gift."

"Can't do that, Sam," Jesse said. "But I will take care of the cow for you until you get up on your feet. With one condition though."

"What's that?"

Friends of the Family

"Cole and I will bring a load of grain and hay over to you next week. We'll see you through this winter. We got a deal?"

Sam hung his head for a few moments.

"That would be a God send, Jesse. Maybe I can do something for you."

"Let me think on it."

"Let's go get warm," Franklin said and they all headed back towards the house.

As they walked up from the barn, Paul and Eddie came tearing out of the house and towards the creek. Lily and Peg were sitting by the fireplace in the front room, playing with Lily's dolls Hattie made for her.

When the men walked into the kitchen, Sarah sat at the huge kitchen table holding one of the babies, as Mary held the other at her breast. They saw Karen setting the table and Hattie was taking some biscuits out of the stove's oven. A pot of white pork gravy was bubbling on the stove.

"Thought you men might like a little biscuits and gravy," Hattie said.

Cole, Mark and the three men sat down and began devouring the food. It felt to Jesse like they'd been friends for a long time and that holding the baby seemed to do wonders for Sarah. They visited and when Hattie served up one of her pumpkin pies she'd been guarding with her life, Jesse knew things were going well.

"I couldn't help noticing those dogs were all sitting in a perfect row when we rode in here," Sam said. "They're huge and mean looking, but appear to be real well mannered. Did you train them?"

"I'm not sure you'll believe me, but they train themselves. See they kind of adopted us, and you'll just have to trust me on this, but you do not want to get them riled up. It's a fearsome sight to see," Jesse said.

"Amen," Franklin said.

"I can believe that. If you don't mind me asking, I noticed both you, and that big dog over there, carry some scars?" Sam asked, pointing at Boss.

"We dealt a few issues when we first got here. The one you're pointing at is Boss. He owns this place and lets us live here. He and the other friends patrol this whole part of the country and generally look out for us. They were bred for that purpose and they're real good at it. That's why we call them friends of the family."

"I just hope they know we were invited here. By the way, what did you and Sarah do before the go-back?" Sam asked.

"I ran a construction company and Sarah was a homemaker. How about you and Mary?"

"I was a policeman over in a small community about forty miles west of Basking Ridge. Mary was a school teacher."

"Mary, you were a school teacher?" Sarah said.

"I taught seventh grade. At least until the checks stopped coming. Sam and I tried to tough it out for a while. When we saw it wasn't going to get better anytime soon, we decided we needed to go back to basics. When we were surprised by the twins, things got a little complicated."

"Surprised?" Hattie asked. "You was surprised? We better talk later, we know what causes that now," Hattie said.

Everyone laughed, but Sarah. Sarah didn't think anything about that subject was funny just now.

chapter 27

WHEN JESSE GOT up the next day it was snowing hard. *There's something magical about the valley when it's draped in a white coat. A beautiful sight, our snowy valley,* Jesse thought. He could hear voices coming from the kitchen.

Hattie and Karen had been up since the crack of dawn and placed several fryers in the oven to slowly bake. The sage dressing added to the mix of smells that made sure no one wandered too far from the kitchen. It was early afternoon when the dinner was finally served. The table groaned under the weight of the food. When the last piece of pie was gone, the men staggered in to sit in front of the fireplace and were fast asleep within minutes.

Sarah said she felt poorly and decided to go lie down for awhile. Hattie and Karen were cleaning up the remnants of the meal while

Cole tried to distract Karen. Mary helped when she could in between feedings. Eddie took Paul out to the barn to teach him how to milk a cow. Paul wasn't looking forward to it, but knew someone needed to learn this, and since no one else volunteered, it was on him to learn.

***

Lily walked quietly past the sleeping forms of Franklin and Sam Scroggins, and tugged on Jesse's sleeve. He opened his eyes and focused on Lily. "What is it honey?"

"I'm not sure, Daddy, but I think something's wrong with Mommy."

Jesse sprang from the chair and headed for the bedroom. "Get Hattie."

Jesse hurried into the bedroom and Sarah was on her side with her legs drawn up. "What's wrong, sweetheart?" Jesse asked softly.

"It's the baby, Jesse. It's early."

Hattie, followed closely by Mary and Lily, sailed into the room.

"Jesse, you clear out of here," Hattie said. "You want to help, go boil a big pot of water."

Jesse fled to the kitchen and put the largest pot of water he could find on the hot stove. Unlike some men, having babies scared the heck out of Jesse. When Mark was born he'd felt the obligation to suggest he be in the delivery room. Sarah knew him well enough to nip that idea in the bud. Jesse retreated to the outer room.

After about an hour, Hattie came into the living room, a concerned look on her face. "Jesse, Sarah's resting as comfortably as she can. We're going to have a baby cause her water broke," Hattie said. "That little thing needed another month or so to cook in her mama, but God says now, so it's now."

"Anything I can do to help?" Jesse asked.

"Just stay out of the way. I've brought thirty babies into this world. Make that thirty one after tonight. You could get me something though."

"Name it."

"I need a length of barn rope, the big thick kind. I need about six or eight feet of it."

"What for?"

"We tie it to the end of the bed. It gives Sarah something to pull on when she gets tired of pushing on her own."

Jesse ran to the barn as fast as he could and cut a length of rope and rushed back to the house. He knocked timidly at the bedroom door. Hattie came out.

"You can't bring that dirty thing into that bedroom. You got a pot of water boiling yet?" Hattie asked.

"Yes," Jesse said.

"Well go put that rope into the boiling water. After awhile, fish it out and you and Franklin pull and twist it to get as much of the water out of it as you can. Then bring it back."

The men washed their hands as if they were going to perform surgery. They boiled and stretched the rope. Franklin and Jesse almost knocked each other down, as they both tried to wedge through the kitchen door at the same time. Hattie was waiting for them, took the rope, and disappeared into the bedroom.

An hour later they heard the unmistakable cries of a newborn baby, coming from the bedroom. Jesse stopped pacing and fell into a chair. Hattie came out a short time later.

"Mother and baby doing just fine, Jesse. The baby girl is a mite small, but she's got all her fingers and toes," Hattie said. "You come on in now, but be quiet and gentle cause Sarah been through a lot."

Jesse followed Hattie back in. Sarah lay in bed with a little pink bundle in her arms.

"It's a girl, Jesse. I named her Jessica," Sarah said sleepily as she closed her eyes.

Friends of the Family

Jesse peeked at the pink little baby's face. Her hair was the color of Sarah's and she had a little frown on her face. She sucked on the tiny little knuckle of her right hand with great purpose.

"She's beautiful, just like her mother," Jesse whispered.

Sarah smiled for a response, without opening her eyes. Jesse kissed her and the baby on the foreheads and left. Lily went to get each of her brothers and escort them in to see their new baby sister.

"Now you be quiet and don't touch anything. You just look and leave," Lily told them. Jesse thought she really was starting to sound more and more like Hattie.

***

The day after baby Jessica was born broke bright and sunny. The Scroggins said good bye and Jesse told them he would see them in a week or so. Two days later Sarah felt strong enough to come out into the living room and sit with the baby. Three days after she was born, baby Jessica became a little jaundiced. Sarah would sit in a rocker with the baby across her lap as the sunlight fell upon the infant's tiny naked body. Jesse stoked up the fireplace and kept the room so hot no one but Sarah and the baby could stand it for long.

Baby Jessica slept fitfully at first and was always hungry. Hattie sat in the kitchen and read her tattered bible. Towards the end of the fourth day, Jessica began sleeping a lot and would cry after her feedings. Sarah sat and rocked baby Jessica for hours, while the tiny infant slept. She hummed or sang little songs that only the infant could hear. She told the baby Jessica all about her life. How she'd met this handsome man who wouldn't take no for an answer, and whom she loved more than life.

Baby Jessica weakened by the sixth day and died on the seventh. It was late afternoon, almost dark, when Jesse walked into the living room. Sarah was rocking baby Jessica and looking out the front window, beyond the porch and the gathering darkness.

"Sarah, would you like me to light a lamp for you?" Jesse asked.

"No, I just want to sit here and hold my baby for a little while longer," Sarah said.

Not a sound was heard except for the creaking of the chair as she continued to rock back and forth, back and forth.

Friends of the Family

"I understand, sweetheart," Jesse said. "I'll be back in a little while. I want to make baby Jessica a nice warm bed."

Jesse walked out onto the back porch and sat down on the step. He looked up at the scattering of stars that were beginning to sprinkle the darkening blue sky from ridge to ridge. Jesse felt a hollow spot deep in his gut he knew wouldn't be filled in this life. He wiped tears from his eyes and sniffed his nose at the cold. The cold always made his eyes water and his nose run. Jesse walked towards the out buildings.

Light was coming from under the door to the woodworking shed. Jesse opened the door and stepped in. Franklin was tenderly working on a small pine box. Jesse saw that it was beautifully crafted with a rose, carved in relief, on the top. Franklin was sanding the outside. Jesse walked up and touched Franklin on the shoulder. Franklin was weeping quietly, his tears falling on the carved rose. Jesse put his hand on Franklin's hand and held it still.

"It's beautiful Franklin," Jesse said. "Baby Jessica needs it now."

Jesse took the box from Franklin and opened it. The box was lined with pink satin in little puffy folds. Jesse put a hand on Franklin's shoulder and squeezed it gently in thanks, and left the shed walking towards the house. Jesse sat at the kitchen table for a while and when the invisible clock said it was time, Jesse took the box to Sarah and baby Jessica.

Sarah stood when Jesse came in and Jesse showed her the box that Franklin made.

"It's so beautiful, Jesse," Sarah said. "Just like baby Jessica."

Sarah took the baby and gently laid her in the pink satin bed.

"Jesse, I want her buried up on the limestone ledge on the south end of the valley," Sarah said. "That's where I want to be buried along side you and this baby."

Jesse nodded and took the box with baby Jessica over to Hattie's where the other adults and children gathered. When he came back Sarah was in bed and fast asleep. She lay with a beautiful smile on her lips and Jesse imagined she dreamed a happy dream, of a small baby named Jessica, who held her finger tightly with tiny pink fingers.

The funeral was held the next day. Hattie read bible passages over the small grave. Sarah was numb with grief. Of all things, Jesse noted that all the friends of the family showed up and sat in a row as if showing their respect.

The others all cried softly as the little box with baby Jessica was placed in the grave and covered with dirt mixed with snow. Franklin had made a grave marker with the same rose as the box. Carved into the marker were the words '*Here lies Baby Jessica. She lives with the Angels.*

***

Jesse and Cole loaded a wagon and made the long trip to the Scroggins place the next week. Sarah was still in bed recovering from the birth and loss of their baby. Jesse and Cole arrived at mid morning and helped Sam unload the wagon.

During a somewhat meager lunch, Jesse asked Sam and Mary if they would consider moving closer to Haven. He explained how they needed help in a number of areas, and how everyone at Haven felt very comfortable with them from their visit.

He told Mary that a small building in Eagle Rock would be converted to a schoolhouse, if she would consider teaching a variety of ages. Mary was enthused by the prospect and Sam was looking forward to being part of Haven. Just before he and Cole left, Jesse passed on the sad news about baby Jessica. Both Sam and Mary took the news hard.

Hattie and Karen did what they could to decorate for Christmas, but knew that it wouldn't be the same without Sarah's help. Still they got through it and winter dragged on. They butchered hogs, two happy frisky colts were born by the end of February, and the first false spring was covered over by a late snowfall. By mid-March, the Scroggins had moved into the next valley, and commuted to Haven each day. April came and Sarah spent a lot of time just walking in the woods. She never noticed the friends that always accompanied her.

***

That spring, on a warm sunny day, Jesse headed from the mill towards the cabins for lunch. As he walked along he saw Sarah sitting by the edge of the creek. He sat down in the grass beside her. Both commented on how they enjoyed the warm sun on their faces and other minor things.

"Jesse?" Sarah finally said. "Would it be the wrong thing to do if we tried for another baby?"

"Sweetheart, how could it possibly be wrong when we love each other so much?" Jesse asked as he took her hand.

"Oh, I don't know. It's just that we were so happy, I think God took baby Jessica just to remind us that life can be hard," Sarah said.

Friends of the Family

Jesse thought about what Sarah said for a while, listening to the babble of the creek running by them.

"Not my God," Jesse finally said. "My God doesn't do things like that. He worries about the big things, and trusts people to sort out the small stuff. The fact is life *is* hard. God knows he doesn't have to point that out. Ask that boy who hid under our pine trees in our front yard a thousand years ago. Cole's now a fine young man of character, who's in love. My God makes sure a beautiful and loving person helps that boy, and loves him as if he were her own. That's how my God gets things done."

Sarah looked at Jesse and smiled.

"Where are you preaching next week?" Sarah asked as she poked Jesse in the ribs.

Jesse poked her back. They wrestled on the bank of the creek. Jesse pinned Sarah beneath him and kissed her hard on the mouth. Sarah kissed him hard in return.

"I love you Mrs. Colter," Jesse said softly.

"I love you, Mr. Colter," Sarah said in return.

Everyone up at the house eating wondered where Jesse and Sarah were, because those two were missing a really good lunch.

chapter 28

SLOWLY THINGS GOT better. Not like before the go-back, but better none the less. Families moved to Eagle Rock and settled. A spirit of community returned. Over the next twenty years, Eagle Rock grew to a point it rivaled Linden in size.

Cole was a major reason for this growth. People had learned, very little could be achieved without justice. Justice applied in a quick and sure fashion. Cole delivered justice. He softened somewhat with his marriage to Karen, the girl he'd brought back to Haven. They raised seven children and lived in a large house. The house sat across the street from an old ruined gas station. At one time it was the only gas station in Eagle Rock, and was on the only street corner in town with a stoplight.

In its day it was considered the best corner in town.

Cole helped Jesse and the others build the only church in Eagle Rock. Cole and Karen's marriage was the first performed in the freshly painted church. The first baptism was theirs as well, a scant five months after the wedding. It was a boy Cole named Herman. When Jesse pointed out the short time period between the two events, Cole was heard to lay the blame on Jesse. He said that if Jesse had built the church quicker, the interval would have been more traditional. In fact the church grew over time, to keep pace with the growth of Eagle Rock. The attendance rose steadily and it rapidly returned to the center of community activity.

Besides the church, the town changed in other ways. The telephone and power lines were gone, as were all the poles that held them. The wire was prized because it was so much tougher than rope. In fact, the wire was easily stretched tight, and made excellent fencing for livestock. The wooden telephone poles were also useful and this contributed to their disappearance. They'd been soaked in creosote and were insect and rot resistant. Creosote made the wood burn with white-hot intensity. It was the blacksmiths who took the telephone poles. They were far superior for heating metal to a workable temperature.

In fact a small industry grew out of the go-back. Those in this industry were called Scrappers. The Scrappers had huge wagons that were pulled by large teams of oxen. They roamed over wide areas, usually in long wagon trains, demolishing and salvaging materials from abandoned towns and villages. In some cases they eliminated most traces of a town, and the weeds and trees did the rest.

Their large buildings, called depots, were in major population centers. They stored the windows, doors, sinks, boards, nails, railings, wire and any other material with real value. If you needed something, and had something to trade, you could usually find what you needed in one of the Scrapper depots.

Jasper Thiggs died in bed. There was talk of putting a statue of Jasper up in the town square, since this brave and good man helped everyone in east Tennessee directly or indirectly. Jasper's son Luther replaced him as the law in Linden. He, like Cole, delivered quick and sure justice. But the general feeling was there could be only the one Jasper. The funeral for him lasted three days as people from far distances continued to pour in to pay their respects.

Finally it was his wife Betty who said "it's time to put old Jasper in the ground, cause all those buzzards are starting to make the horses nervous." Betty continued to serve the best pie within fifty miles of Linden. It may have been further, but few people traveled that far.

Sam and Mary Scroggins moved from Haven to Eagle Rock after a while, so Mary could be closer to the school she taught. People had forgotten some of the advantages of a one-room schoolhouse. Older children were called upon to help the younger ones, and learned more as a result. Sam and Mary's daughter Peg joined her mother as a teacher, and the school expanded as frequently as the church. School breaks were aligned with the seasons to help with the planting and harvesting of crops.

While the lessons were focused on reading, writing and arithmetic, an extensive library was constructed next to the school. The library grew since the scrappers made sure that they saved every book they found. They furnished them to the libraries for free. Sam and Mary's oldest boy, Eddie, continued to work with his dad in the Colter lumber business. Zack and Zeke grew straight and strong and were a

Friends of the Family

constant source of confusion since no one beyond the Scroggins could tell them apart.

Mark and Paul grew closer over the years as their age difference narrowed, as it always seems to do with age. Mark ran the logging business and Paul ran the mill. The businesses and brothers were forever linked. The lumbering business expanded as more and more people moved into the area. Finally, the brothers opened a lumberyard in Eagle Rock and another in Linden. They were ranging farther and farther from Haven for lumber, and on one such trip Mark met a lovely young woman named Susan.

She proved to be a major distraction to Mark, and business suffered for a while. The brothers built a cabin for Susan and Mark right next to the Colter main house. The marriage of Mark and Susan was a significant event in the growing town of Eagle Rock. Cole was Mark's best man and Jesse gave the bride away because Susan's father was dead.

The newlyweds moved into the cabin and soon after, Susan began to show signs of new life. The first grandchild arrived a short time later. It was a boy and Mark named the boy Jesse Junior Colter. His father asked Mark why he named the boy Jesse Junior.

Joel Baker

"Why, so we can call him JJ," Mark replied with a smile.

Paul loved working with the water wheel and mill. He seldom went anywhere far from their operation. Sarah and Hattie started to worry whether Paul would ever get far enough away from it to find a bride of his own. It turned out that they'd worried for nothing. The sister of the man they hired to run the lumberyard in Linden set her cap for Paul. Her name was Julie and Paul was in awe of her from the beginning.

"Paul never stood a chance," Hattie said, when Paul told his folks the good news. "She would have done anything to trap that boy."

"Now, Hattie. It wasn't two months ago, you were worried that Paul would be a bachelor his whole life," Jesse reminded her.

"Well in my day, she would have been referred to as brazen," Hattie muttered as she huffed out of the kitchen.

Jesse, Paul, and Mark began construction of the new cabin for Paul and Julie right beside Mark and Susan's. Haven grew and so did the Colter extended family. Paul and Julie proved to be frequent contributors, with five children in seven years.

Lily grew to be a lovely woman with her mother's figure and her daddy's coloring.

Friends of the Family

When she was seventeen, Hattie noticed the way she brightened, whenever Eddie Scroggins was over helping his dad and Paul with the mill. Certainly Sam noticed that his son was way too eager to help over at Haven. Once in a while Eddie would hang around until dinner was ready. He and Lily would go for a walk after dinner. Sarah and Mary Scroggins considered the possibilities this presented and both stopped just short of being accused of meddling by Jesse and Sam, but not by much.

***

Late one evening, Jesse was sitting on the front porch rocking in his chair with Boss at his side, when Eddie rode up and climbed off his horse. He sat on the front steps by Jesse and Boss.

"Mr. Colter, I'd like your daughter's hand in marriage. I love her, and she loves me. I'm a hard worker and a Christian, and I'd make her a good husband," Eddie said in an obviously over-rehearsed speech.

Jesse looked hard at him and continued to rock back and forth for a while. The tension grew as Jesse and Boss both stared at Eddie. Long after the silence grew awkward, Jesse stopped rocking.

"Boy, you ever lay a hand on my daughter in anger, Boss and I will hunt you down and you better pray to God that I find you before Boss does."

Eddie listened closely to what Jesse said. He thought about it for a few moments.

"Is that a yes?" Eddie asked, somewhat confused.

"Why, I guess it is," Jesse said with a smile.

"Thank you, Mr. Colter. I'll make her a good and loving husband."

Jesse got up and walked into the house. Sarah and Lily were sitting in the kitchen trying to look busy.

"Lily, there's someone on the front porch who wants to talk to you, I believe," Jesse said.

Lily jumped to her feet, gave her dad a hug, and ran for the front porch. Jesse poured himself a cup of coffee and sat down at the table next to Sarah.

"I can't believe Lily's going to marry someone with the last name of Scroggins. I always thought that was the ugliest last name I ever heard," Jesse said, shaking his head.

"Would you have preferred Luther Thiggs," Sarah said.

Friends of the Family

"Hummm, Lily Thiggs. Maybe Scroggins isn't such a bad name after all," Jesse said, as both he and Sarah began to laugh.

***

The wedding took place in Eagle Rock three weeks after Eddie and his dad finished the cabin just up the creek from the rest of the Colter houses. Jesse gave Lily away, but couldn't help feeling melancholy about the whole thing.

Sarah and Hattie made the wedding gown, with Hattie complaining the whole time about how there was no way that a Scroggins was good enough for her Lily, and how she would probably never see her again and so on. When Hattie found out Lily and Eddie would only be living a couple of hundred yards away, she took to the idea with more enthusiasm.

It was late, the night of the wedding, after the last guests departed. Sarah and Jesse stood on their front porch and watched the newlyweds walk hand and hand up the East Ridge road to their new cabin.

"I'm feeling very old right now," Jesse said.

"I know. This is when I miss baby Jessica most," Sarah said.

"Me too," Jesse said. "Me too."

***

Cole and his family were frequent visitors at Haven. His children played and swam with the Colter children. His wife, Karen, became a daughter to Jesse and Sarah, just as Cole was their son.

Cole gained a bit of a reputation as someone not to mess with. He continued to wear the long brown coat Sarah for him made so many years ago. He started wearing a holster and pistol and was renowned as lightning quick and deadly accurate. Cole was welcomed wherever he ranged in pursuit of people who robbed or murdered simple folk.

No one, beyond Karen and Jesse, could understand or explain the relentless determination of Cole. People would marvel at how he never gave up once he took to someone's trail. Both decent folk and outlaws wondered at Cole's persistence.

Karen knew Cole better than anyone. She knew how Jesse and Sarah had taken Cole in at the time of the move. She knew they loved him like a son. Cole always avoided questions about that time, and discussions about his parents. One day while cleaning out a junk drawer, Karen came across an old faded and crinkled photo. At first glance Karen thought it was Cole with another woman and a little boy holding on to his leg. Karen was taken back by the resemblance between Cole and his father and the stoic look on the little boy's face.

Franklin died fifteen years to the day after the Colters arrived in Haven. He'd been working in the north end of the valley all morning. Hattie went out and rang the dinner bell for lunch. The grandchildren and Jesse arrived in a rush. Sarah and Hattie served up a farmer's lunch. Slices of ham, with green beans and fresh corn on the cob were served on big platters. Potato salad and big glasses of sun tea chilled in the creek completed lunch. Franklin still hadn't arrived.

Jesse asked JJ, Mark's oldest boy, to go get him. Franklin was known to fall asleep in the fields lately, so nobody worried. When Jesse saw the boy riding hard towards the house, he knew something was wrong.

"Grandpa Jesse. Come quick. Something's awful wrong with Franklin," JJ said.

Jesse climbed up behind JJ and rode to where Franklin laid in what appeared to be a peaceful sleep with a gentle smile on his lips. Jesse knelt down by his best friend.

"Franklin?" Jesse said as he shook him gently.

Jesse leaned over and put his ear on Franklin's chest. When he knew the great heart was stilled, Jesse took Franklin in his arms and held him close for a few moments. *Good bye old friend.*

Tears filled his eyes. Jesse lifted Franklin and placed him over the horse. He and JJ led the horse and Franklin back to Hattie.

Hattie took to her cabin for several days and refused to attend the funeral. She told Sarah she wanted to send Franklin off in her own way, but asked that certain passages from the Bible be read over him. Hattie made a special effort to comfort Jesse, who took Franklin's death hard. Jesse and Sarah agreed that Hattie was the strongest person they'd ever known.

For Hattie's part, she took an increased interest in Lily, and her education in the use of plants and medicine. No one but Hattie knew that in the still dark hours of the pre-morning, she would roam all around Haven and remember times past. She would think about her own stillborn babies, and her regrets about not having children to comfort her in her old age.

Then she would smile and cry at the memory of her Franklin and the joy she felt when she considered they'd be together again, once she also crossed over the river Jordan. She'd have babies then, lots and lots of babies.

chapter 29

JESSIE COLTER IS dying and he's okay with that. The uninvited dark clump in his gut is a welcomed guest. It's time, and Jessie feels complacent. He's an old man with a bent back and sore joints sitting on an oak tree stump, in front of a fire, in a small flat clearing on the side of a mountain in Tennessee. It was a cold dreary afternoon in late November.

The old man's gray hair hangs down to his shoulders. It covers the collar of his long brown canvas coat. His rifle rests across his knees. The odd-shaped blanket around his shoulders was the first result of the family's experiment with weaving on a rickety hnad made loom.

Jesse lifts his head and gazes out over the panoramic vista of mountain ridges. They're covered with pine, birch hickory, ash, oak, beechnut and slippery elm trees that wave the last of their brown leaves in the occasional westerly breeze. Below lays Haven. A valley with the quick-flowing stream, lined with cabins that house his family and the friends of the family.

Jesse and Sarah had built the community almost thirty years ago. No longer threatened, and self-sufficient, Jesse feels a sense of inner-peace. Finally, he's free to join his beloved wife, Sarah.

The day lengthens, and the cold mountain breeze with its icy fingers reaches out and stirs his hair. The breeze ebbs and flows through the tree leaves, sounding like gentle surf hitting a distant shore. Icy fingers squeeze Jesse's neck, sending chills down his back. It smells of snow. The gray clouds lower, and darken to the color of a gray slate chalkboard at their edges. He moves closer to the fire and clutches the lumpy blanket around his shoulders more tightly. He studies his scarred and leathered hands.

"Jesse, when did you become an old man?" he says out loud, to nobody.

Jesse remembers everything and nothing. He always said he'd been hit on the head one too many times. But he is sharp enough. It's just that his memory plays tricks on him. Sometimes he can remember long ago times. Like how the spider web in the corner of the corn-

Friends of the Family

crib looked, in the early morning, when it was still covered with small drops of dew.

Let's see, that was when I was six. I moved from Haven to live with Aunt Rose when I was...I know it was after my parents died...

Jesse lives in the twilight now. He knows why they call them the twilight years. A dewy summer's morning is clear. What he ate for dinner last night, isn't. Jesse shivers and is back on the mountain. He sits in front of a fire with a view to all the land that makes up Haven. A cascade of mountains marches toward the lowering gray sky. Row after row of blue hills are shrouded in a cold gray mist. The scent of pine trees and the acrid smell of smoke from Jesse's fire mingle.

The cold always makes my eyes water and my nose run.

He sniffs, and wipes his nose with a bright red bandana.

Sarah thought it was because he had his nose broken so many times. *"Won't you ever learn to duck?"* Jesse smiles to himself, remembering. His eyes water some more. This time, it isn't from the cold.

He slowly scans the valley from right to left. Far below is a cluster of cabins that are weathered gray.

Like the people in the Colter family, the cabins and buildings were added as they came. They followed the stream snaking through the valley. They were tough and equal to whatever came their way. The family, and the cabins that sheltered them, endured. They were rough-looking on the outside, but filled with warmth and a glow. They were resolved to see it through, to shelter those in need. The cabins, and the people they sheltered, were very much alike.

When they'd first come to Haven only a couple of cabins and some sheds sat in the central part of the valley along the stream. They'd been serviceable, but run down with thirty years of neglect. Brown lumps sitting along a bubbling creek, in the green sea of grass that occupied the center of the valley. An old shack clung to the side of the west ridge about half way down, and could barely be seen in amongst the bramble bushes and lodge pole pines that engulfed it.

***

When Sarah had slowed and fallen ill a little over year ago, Jesse had been on a trip with the friends of the family. While Jesse was gone, Sarah grew worse. One by one, she said goodbye to all her children and grandchildren, then waited for Jesse to return. When Jesse finally rode slowly up, dismounted, and tied his reins to the porch post, he'd sensed something was wrong. Lily came out on the front porch and dabbed her eyes with her hanky.

"Daddy, I think Momma's crossing over," Lily said in hushed tones.

"Honey, where is she?"

"She's in the back bedroom waiting for you."

Jesse slowly climbed the steps, crossed the porch, took his hat in his hands, and entered the cool dark interior of the cabin. He stood for a while and let his eyes adjust to the pale light filtering through the windows. Jesse thought if he took his time, Sarah might live a while longer. He walked slowly to the back bedroom door. Still a tall man, Jesse ducked his head and entered the room with sunlight filtering through the lacey curtains that hung in the windows.

Jesse couldn't breathe. Sarah lay on the bed. But not the Sarah he'd kissed goodbye a week ago. This was the Sarah he knew thirty years ago. Her hair was a rich brown. Her face was unlined and unwrinkled. Her lips were full and red. The smooth sheet revealed the soft curves that Jesse remembered so vividly. On her face the sweet look of sleep. Jesse started to cry silently.

"Jesse, is that you?"

"Yes, darling it's me."

"Come over and give me a kiss good-bye."

"Where are you going?"

I'm not really sure where. But I know that when I get there, I got a sweet little baby that wants to grow up, waiting for me."

"I'm going with you."

"In a little while Jesse, but not right now." Sarah coughed weakly. "You got little ones to be grandpa to. The boys need your advice for a while more. When you're done with that, you come be with me. Come on over here."

Jesse walked across the room and sat on the edge of the bed. He now saw the illusion that startled him when he'd first entered the room. Sarah had someone, probably Lily, touch up her hair with a dye made from walnut husks. Her skin was relaxed and showed no sign of age. The sheet covering her form didn't lie. Jesse smiled at Sarah.

"Had you going when you first came in, didn't I?" Sarah gave Jesse her old mischievous grin.

"You sure did, girl."

Friends of the Family

"Well, if I left before you got back, I didn't want your last sight of me to be some gray-haired old woman."

"Darling, it wouldn't have mattered. I've loved you with my whole heart for fifty years. I found my soul mate, my lover, all those years ago. Even last week, when we kissed goodbye, I saw the sweet beauty of my youth. When my time comes, I'll only know for sure I'm in heaven, when I see you walking slowing to meet me, with that swing in your hips and the love in your eyes."

Sarah smiled lovingly into Jesse's eyes, too weak to speak. Holding each other's hands, both tried to hold that moment in time, forever. Jesse kissed Sarah as if for the last time. It was.

Jesse's eyes watered up again. As he leaned over Sarah, a single tear dropped lightly onto her cheek. Jesse kissed each of her eyes and her still warm lips. His teardrop ran slowly down Sarah's cheek. Jesse sat and held Sarah's hand gently as the light filtering through the lacy curtains dimmed to dark.

***

After the funeral, Jesse went away for a while. He went to his spot on the side of the mountain where he could see all of Haven. The friends of the family checked on him from time to time. They made sure no one bothered him. He barely noticed their silent coming and going.

He sat for days and thought of his life with Sarah. That's when he first noticed a twinge in his stomach. It was a small sharp pain that promised a great deal more. Occasionally at night, when the wind blew through the lodge pole pines, they whispered a message to Jesse. The boughs would creak and rasp as they rubbed together and the needles would sing softly.

One morning Jesse stood, put the embers of his fire out with water from the spring near where he sat, and walked down the mountain. Family and friends consoled him, and Jesse frequently went on trips with the friends. The requests from the little ones for the family story were more frequent, as if they sensed something. Days turned to weeks, weeks to months, and fall arrived. He spent more and more time sitting on his spot on the mountain. He sits there now.

The uninvited guest in Jesse shoots a small bolt of pain through his gut. Jesse figures the guest just wants to remind him from time to time. Just a little notice to Jesse that he'll be with Sarah before the snow melts and the Mountain Holly is in bloom.

Friends of the Family

As an omen of things to come, it begins to snow. Light flakes, occasional flakes fall in meandering paths drifting slowly left, then right. As the first flakes touch the earth, they pause then slowly melt. Each flake giving its life to cool the earth, so other flakes survive. One flake, perhaps bolder than the rest, perhaps a simple matter of fortunate timing, clings to a single blade of grass and refuses to let go. It waits to see if it will live. A second flake joins the first. They wait together. A third joins, then a forth, a fifth.

The collection becomes a dusting, then a covering. A white blanket runs down the sides of the mountain. It covers the roofs of the cabins below, the cords of firewood stacked high against the walls, the dead rusted shell of a truck, and the barnyard where the horses stand side by side and peer up with dull wonder at the falling snow.

Jesse sees the door of the main cabin open and a large man with a bushy beard walks out on the porch and stretches. He's wearing a long brown canvas coat reaching nearly to the ground, just like the one Jesse wears. His hat's pulled down on his ears and he looks up at the falling snow. Emerging from the door behind the man, appear the friends of the family.

They walk out in single file and sit in an orderly row. Jesse recognizes his oldest son Mark, almost fifty now. The large black dogs look up at Mark with golden eyes and close attention.

Mark kneels by the largest dog. He lays his hand on the dog's head and says something. The dog rises and trots off at a leisurely gait. The remaining dogs stay at Mark's side. Jesse follows the first dog's progress as he trots toward, then up the mountain path. The path leads to where Jesse sits in front of a fire, being slowly smothered by a blanket of snow.

As the dog comes up the path, it disappears and reappears from behind rock outcroppings and trees. When the dog reaches a relatively level surface, Jesse notes that one of it's legs appears injured. It's Boss. Jesse named the dog after the first Boss, the obvious leader of the friends all those years ago.

Jesse watches the dog make steady progress up the path, and as expected, he vanishes as he approaches the clearing where Jesse sits. The friends seldom approached you from where you expect. Instead they disappear behind a rock, a shrub, a tree, a stand of tall grass. They were seldom seen, unless they wanted to be.

Friends of the Family

Jesse waits. The snow continues. Slowly the hairs on the back of his neck begin to rise and Jesse looks over his shoulder. Boss sits staring silently. His sleek black coat is slick with wet snow. His golden eyes fixed on Jesse's back. Boss sits down and lays his massive head on his leg.

Jesse knows Mark sent the dog to fetch him, but he's in no hurry. He watches the smoke continue to rise from the cabins below, blue-gray blending with the lowering clouds. The smell of acrid smoke from his dying campfire recalls good memories. He leans forward and pats the dog's head.

Jesse listens to the wind in the pines. They haven't whispered to him in quite some time. Instead, Jesse hears the faint ticking of that invisible clock. It's slowly ticking as he waits on the side of a mountain, for the snow to melt and the Mountain Holly to bloom.

Made in the USA
Lexington, KY
04 June 2013